GYPSY

ROVERS

By

Kathleen W. FitzGerald

Whales' Tale Press, First Printing, 2020.

ISBN: 979-8-657-26592-7 (Paperback)

Any references to historical events, real people, or real
places are used fictitiously. Names, characters, and
places are products of the author's imagination.

First printing edition 2020.

Whales' Tale Press
P.O. Box 144
Lake Villa, IL 60046

Cover illustration by Anne FitzGerald, Studio/Gallery
in Mungret College, Limerick, Ireland.

Book and cover design by Phalen J. Wiegold.

Dedicated to the sweet Memory of

Tommy, Sean, and Garrett

Joy to the Dreams of

Phalen, Cián, Annie and Bridget

With Heartfelt Gratitude to:

Anne FitzGerald, for her beautiful painting
of *Poulnabrone Dolman,* Burren, Co. Clare, for the
cover of Gypsy Rovers

Bri'd McMahon for her continual hospitality to her
lovely home in Corofin, the Burren.

Tom FitzGerald who patiently and kindly
negotiated the cyber-space rapids that I was quite
unable to shoot

Dee Christie (Dr. Dolores L.) who scrupulously
edited my drafts with a hammer in one hand and a
feather in the other

Phalen Wiegold who artistically and wisely
designed the entire manuscript

The Blue Birds who sang to me when I grew faint
of heart

Congregations, out of step with contemporary life,

plodding painfully along on the fringe of the world's development,

are an anachronism.

The Nun in the World (1963)

Leon Joseph Cardinal Suenens

Table of Contents

Preamble

AD 2048

Molly was walking gingerly across the rickety, wobbly bridge that crossed the Shannon River in Killaloe, the sweetest town in the world.

Sometimes the water meandered, sometimes it rushed, just like us folks. Molly had an ache in her heart, not a horrible pain as if someone had died, but we were all dead now anyhow.

So much of her history had been washed away, memory and dreams as thin as the ripples in the Shannon, only to be carried away in the one continual stream from one end of the country to the other.

She rested her hands against the top of the bridge and rested her face on top of her hands. Her gaze took in the young cattails, stretching to the sun, a wounded green turtle turning blue, and sheltering the fish from the current was a crumpled fisherman's hat, entwined in the reeds and tall blades of grass.

Molly felt as if she were pushed from the bridge. She tore down the walkway and around the posts, trying to gain a foothold as she slipped down the embankment. She reached into the dark waters for the hat, calling to her deepest heart beats.

She placed the hat over her head, holding the sides so it would not leave her. She took the hat off, lifting it ever so gently from her head. Trapped in the lining were three long red hairs, saved for her from her aunt Winnie.

Chapter One

The Beginning of the End

Oh, Sweet Jesus, there she goes again! She sneaks out every day when they are not closely watching her. "Sister Brigid!! It is only me, Fiona Flaherty! Where are you?"

"WHERE ARE THE YOUNG NUNS??? WHERE ARE THEY? WHY ARE THEY HIDING FROM ME? WHERE ARE THE YOUNG NUNS? I CAN'T FIND THEM!!!!!"

Poor Sister Brigid Mary!! Oh, God love her so!! I had better go get her and bring her back to St. Luke's. The nurses will be looking for her. On my way!

I cannot figure that out. She was a brilliant, brilliant woman, pled cases before the Supreme Court. She still wears her white habit and black veil, as her body and mind are stuck in 1968. Oh, the poor little thing. Down deep, I know if I were older, I would be just like her, shouting and screaming for the young nuns who left us and are far away or never entered the convent in the first place.

My work on earth is almost finished and I hope the Good Lord is getting anxious to see me. I pray every day for a "soft landing" when I sail into the Mystic. As we have aged so quickly, the superiors have brought us back up to where this all began, to our Motherhouse for our care and comfort.

So now we have been brought back to finish up our days. Sometimes we feel like we are in a cattle round-up, nervous, frantic, bumping into each other as our days are few. We still call it "The Motherhouse". It is a beautiful stone castle up in the rolling hills and deep valleys of central Wisconsin, smack between the roaring, mighty Mississippi, and the treachery of deep and dark Lake Michigan.

It was on these very lands, so many years ago, that the French Jesuits sought out the Menominee, the Chippewas, the Ho-Chunks, the Potawatomi to offer them the Sacraments.

We are much closer to Chicago than Milwaukee. Chicago was called *shikaakwa,* the French version of the Indian name for the wild onion. Most of our ministry was in Illinois, rather than Wisconsin. In the onion fields of Chicago, I labored.

Most of us entertain the aches and pains we never thought possible when we were just kids, learning how to be nuns. Some of us are still scattered among the cities and towns where we worked, unwilling to terminate their ministry until the end is finally in sight.

I thought my work was finished, but now that I can rest a bit, I feel like a strong and long cobalt-blue marlin, going into the warm and shallow waters to eat. I thought I was heading back down to the deep and cold waters where I make my home; the soft and easy way is not for me.

This is the first time in my life that I don't have my ears to the ground, listening for bells, whistles, gongs, knocks, buzzers, chimes or sirens to get me on my way, without a thought, just in the spirit of Obedience, Pavlovian dogs salivating at the first peal of his bell. It has taken me a while to simply breathe, close my eyes and to give my poor ears a quiet rest.

On the long, white marble halls up to our beautiful chapel walls were black framed 8 x 10 pictures of the Irish prelates we served throughout the country: bishops, archbishops, cardinals, priors, abbots, monsignors, papal emissaries. No women.

Sometimes I would think of the thoroughbreds, two- and three-year-olds, at the horse sales in Lexington, Kentucky at the Keeneland Auctions. These prestigious churchmen, picking out the fillies whom they wanted to fill their own stables. I never made eye-contact with any of them.

The polished white terrazzo led us right into chapel where we filled the rafters with our soft chanting the hours of the Office of the Blessed Virgin. *"Laeta'tus sum in his quae dicta sunt mihi: In domum Do'mini i'bimus."*

Latin was the language of the church. It always seemed to me to be masculine with clear rules and consistent endings, marching us right along as the men decided where and how we should be. Not like the French or Irish which is more invitational.

The life of Mary, the Mother of God, surrounded us in stained-glass windows, high up on the walls, the brilliant colors spilling over like faraway rainbows when the sun comes out. When we chanted the Office, we faced each other across the entire nave of the chapel and chanted away! Almost like *Titanic* survivors on opposite boats, waving and shouting good-bye.

The glass was stained red as blood, blue - deep and wonderous as a cold night sky, and yellows and whites as pure as the small round beach stones, cuddling together on the warm sand, and the greens would again take you again across the seas to that little island of the 40 shades of green.

We slept on narrow, lumpy cots in our huge damp dormitories, like young soldiers, the first time away from home. Some of us would be talking in our sleep, a few were crying with homesickness, snoring, tossing thin blankets or flimsy pillows at the monsters knocking on our rattling glass windows.

The first part of our preparation to be a real nun was called the Postulancy. We wore a thin, black veil over our natural hair, a black blouse and skirt, black stockings and shoes, with white plastic cuffs and a plastic collar. We were semi-nuns who were sent home if the superiors thought we did not have what it takes to be nuns or if we just wanted to leave. Our group got reduced almost in half.

7

After a year of being postulants, we became novices with the new habit consisting of a tunic, a long, loose dress that hung from our neck to the floor, gathered with a leather belt from which we hung our 15-decade rosary and a small leather holster for our watch and pen. The sleeves were long and loose and required pinning before we wore it.

Over the tunic we placed the scapular that hung from the front and back. We kissed this article of clothing before putting it on. The veil was white when we became novices, signifying that we had not yet made our vows at this time. The novitiate lasted from one to two years, depending upon the choice of each order.

I felt so wonderful in my new habit, but it took some getting used to. We did not know whether to lift our skirts in the front or the back. One new nun in our "crowd" lifted the back of her tunic going down a steep flight of wooden stairs, fell down the stairs and knocked out her two front teeth. I remember that crash that shook the windows.

At this time, we moved into smaller dormitories with white curtains on rods circling our cots. An illusion of privacy. Every night before the lights went out, the superior would come to each of us and bless our cots with a small, silver bucket of holy water.

I had discovered a very old, tightly wrapped bit of pink bubble-gum. I'd chew it at night, blow myself some nice, big bubbles and when the lights went out, I'd plop the blob on the head my little plastic statue of the Blessed Virgin, nice and neat, like a bowler hat that the ladies in Bolivia wear.

One evening I was in bed, before the lights went out, propped up on my pillow, blowing my nice, pink bubbles. The superior came by to bless my bed with her holy water and spied me behind my pink bubble.

She held her head high, clicking her heels and marching right on to the next novice. She did not make eye contact with me the next day. I never apologized because there was not a rule against blowing bubbles in bed. I did not want to get scrupulous.

I could never count all the little First Graders I have taught for years and years; the Walking Wounded adults I have cared for in their therapeutic struggles; the nuns, my sisters, creating community and service as needed. And millions of prayers for my own family of blood, the Flahertys.

Lest I seem too lofty in my pursuits, neither could I count all the meals I cooked, all the toilets I have scrubbed, the tears I have swallowed, the miles I have ridden.

At the beginning, we thought everything was unchangeable, just like the church. We would be wearing the dead nuns' habits and veils, teaching school, kneeling to ask basic permissions until the day we died.

Did our vows go the way of our habits? Are we up here to save our families the cost of burying us, or are we here to receive from the Lord the gift of our final days in a renewed and wiser spirit of Poverty, Chastity and Obedience?

Oh, Dear Mother of God! Little Brigit, Mary of the Gaels, is now swinging the old garage door open to find the hiding places for the new non-existent nuns.

Sister Brigid could simply not comprehend that there were no more nuns. They left us by the hundreds to get married, start a family, live a more non-predictive life.

Every time I get word that someone I knew is marrying a priest or any other man, I feel anxious. I cannot figure out how long sex takes, and I have no one to ask. I wish them the best and try not to think of them having sex.

Chapter Two

Winnie O

Sometimes it is nicer to clasp my old rosary beads than to say them. The ones that my niece brought me back from Ireland were too hard for my fingers. I just like my soft, old black wooden ones the best, not that hard, green Irish marble.

Sweet Heart of Jesus, she is here again. "Winnie O, just come in."

"Fiona, dear, how ye' be in this fine day in March? Are you trying to keep the Fast for Lent? My nerves are at me again, and as much as I would love not to be eating, I know I cannot do that, not at our age.

We entered the convent that same September day, the 6th, in 1956. Winnie O got stuck with her name, as our Postulant Mistress, would shout for her: "Winifred O'Brien! Winifred O'Boyle! Winifred O'Grady!" And we would all look to the back door of our Community Room, and Winnie O would come sliding in after all of us had been sitting there for 20 minutes. In Silence.

We all started out at our proverbial 'base camp', the Motherhouse. And this is where we have all ended up, right where we started. Over half of our Crowd has either died or left many years ago.

Before the big exodus in the early 70's, nuns would be sent home, literally, in the dark of night. If someone were getting in trouble or causing trouble with others, she would be gone in the flash of an eye. Her "nun clothes" folded up neatly on her chair, sheets and blankets doubled over, not even her shadow remained.

After a year of being a postulant, we received our religious habits and our new religious names. Winifred O'Grady receive "Sr. Mary Winifred" as her new religious name. While the rest of us were thrilled that our dreams were coming true, Winnie O was heart-broken that she'd have to carry that horrible name for the rest of her life.

I looked up St Winifred in a huge, Catholic Saints book and found out that *St. Winifred of Wales* had rejected the sexual advances of a dirty, old man and he chopped off her head. It was quickly restored by the Lord and a Healing Spring sprang forth, just like in Lourdes.

13

Winnie O wanted *Sr. Mary Incarnata* for her new religious name. I'd tell her all the time, "Now, Winnie, who'd want to spend their life being the "fourth principle part of the verb, *incarnare*?" (I was a Latin major!) She would stick her thumb downward and I would smile back, so sweetly.

Winnie and I are first cousins. Our mothers were sisters and we lived next door to the O'Gradys our whole lives. My auntie was Flossie O'Grady and she was the sister of my mother, Ellie Flaherty. They were called 'Florence' and 'Helen' by their mother, our grandmother, who we just called Grannie.

Both Flossie and Ellie had six kids each: Paul O'Grady, married to Flossie, was a depressed, unsuccessful engineer; my father was Peter Flaherty, a lawyer and gambler. Best combination in the world: a lawyer and a gambler! Yes, and he drank!

If it were not for our grandfather, Patrick Plunkett, we would have all gone hungry. He died of a stroke on Good Friday, but he made lots of money in his pub where he would sell the Irish Sweeps, like old lottery tickets.

Winnie told me that he kept his girlfriend, Rosie Walsh, down the basement of the tavern.

One night, Grannie Plunkett, 'all dolled up', took the streetcar down to Plunkett's Café, ordered all the drinkers out, stormed down the steps, chased Rosie back up the stairs with her black umbrella and told her husband "No More!" Grandpa Patrick barely got his trousers buttoned before Grannie's appearance.

***

Winnie is sitting at the end of my bed. In about 20 seconds she'll have her pale blue eyes looking out the window, watching, just watching what is going on down at the cemetery, where the dead nuns are all planted in concentric circles, starting in the year 1873.

Winnie is a woman of the earth, of food, children, jokes, tears, and hysteria. She had no time for *paradigms, algorithms,* or *theoretical constructs.* She was built close to the earth, her ruddy-red hair flowed to her eyebrows and eye lashes, so her light blue eyes cast hypnotic images when she looked at you. She never understood how she rattled her listeners.

15

Winnie felt that there was little difference between plants and trees, dolphins and goldfish, cats and dinosaurs, and us humans. "We all come from the bloody hand of God. Just read the beginning of the Bible and that's all you need to know!"

"Winnie, how many circles are going around down there now?"

"Fiona, you know that as well as I do. 16 circles. Good nuns or bad, fat or thin, smart or dumb, sick or well, Irish or more Irish. Oh, I think Regina and Jude are racing each other now!"

"Do you know what you're talking about? Sick, definitely — no well nuns get buried in St. Joseph Cemetery." So often I lost it with Winnie and her mythology.

"Do you like being cousins, Fiona?"

"Isn't it a little late in the day for this type of thinking, Winnie?"

"Don't be so hard on me, Fiona. Not a day goes by without a crack from you, do you know that? I have probably been a rock around your neck forever. You

16

always wanted to be with the smart nuns, and you got stuck with me."

"Winnie, this is going nowhere. Every day I have to keep telling you that I love you and I wouldn't have another cousin hanging from my neck except for you."

"You're so good to me, Fiona. I heard Grannie telling you to keep an eye out for me when we were getting ready to go in the convent. Then I knew you would always have my back."

"Winnie, you are driving me stark-raving crazy! You are a grown woman, three months older than me and you have taken care of yourself for 53 years. You have taught thousands of kids and lived with hundreds of nuns. Please do not start selling yourself short, Winnie. You are my favorite nun-cousin!"

"They're all jumping and dancing around down there. Not a care in the world, Fiona, not like us, draggin' these old bodies around like dead horses from the Galway Races."

I know I am getting short with Winnie. Fifty-five years away from home and we are still joined at the hip. I

17

know it was in the Holy Mind of the Good Lord that we stick together from the first moments we were born. And together both of us have put in over 100 years in His Service.

What is starting to scare me is that I am getting that old itchy feeling that I have got to get the hell out of here. We are all just sitting around waiting to croak.

But what we have here are old ladies who would never dream of leaving. We have hot meals, friends, nurses and doctors, cars, Masses and rosaries, TV, funerals galore with a little nip after they are laid in their cold, cold graves. I am bored to tears. I am choking on my tears. My tears are blinding me.

We are so lucky to be here. When I think of all those old people sleeping in the street, eating out of dumpsters, the dogs and cats after them, running from doctors and nurses, scratching around for a buck or so, depressed and planning to kill themselves if they can figure where to do it.

We still have our vows of poverty, but we want for nothing. The sisters in our families never say a word against us, but I know damn well what they're thinking, with Uncle Paul out of work most of the time and my father Peter Flaherty gambling and drinking up every cent his brilliant mind can squeeze out of the legal system.

We avoided all that chaos that a family makes just by being themselves. They all have financial troubles, their health, academics, the church, nerves, and depressions. I have noticed how few wrinkles are on our faces, compared to our sisters and cousins at home.

But our chaos was down deep, within the four walls of our flesh and blood, our soul and history and prayer and rage and love for the whole world. Our world here is so circumscribed, so tight around me, I must slap myself in the face just to remember to breathe. I am exhausted from living, breathing, being.

Mostly, I miss my ministry. Here we are just receiving the generous services of the many people who have been hired to help us as we age. There is plenty of life left in us two old nuns, and the both of us are simply aching to give it away!

Chapter Three

Our Wild, Winsome Dreamings

Winnie and I did not make eye-contact all throughout dinner. I sat with a poor, older sister who is completely blind, and we take turns cutting her food and wiping her chin. I sensed Winnie was following me into chapel for night prayers. I just could not get away from that woman.

"Fiona, I've known you for 73 years and I know damn well you are cooking something up in that devious mind of yours"

"Let me go up to your room with you, Winnie. You are right as rain. Let us just go!"

We took the elevator up to the 3rd Floor and Winnie whipped out her keys, opened her door, and guided me to her big red rocker by the window. She sat on her bed. I asked her if she still had our habits from the old days when we were garbed from head to foot.

The word *habit* refers to any color of religious clothing worn by both men and women. I first thought it was called that because you got so used to wearing those clothes, that it became a "habit".

Unique clothing becomes iconic, like uniforms for the military, white dresses and caps for nurses, veils for nuns, plain uniforms for Catholic school kids. You tell the world what you are about by the clothes on your back.

With a smile like she had when she mastered the Ten Commandments in Fourth Grade, Winnie knelt on the floor and with the grace of a turtle, slowly drew out Grannie's old black bag from under her bed.

With a rapid glance to check that the door was locked, she unzipped the bag and there, as if no one had ever touched it, lay our old habits, immaculate, ironed to a crisp.

Our habits were the long dresses with loose sleeves that formed the basis of what we wore. On top of that we would put our scapular over our heads, another long fabric, running down the front and back. In the side pockets of Grannie's bag were our thick, black belts and our 15-decade rosaries, weights to steady us on the path to the Lord.

21

My knees grew weak and my heart thrashed in my chest like a wild *bodhran*, that flat Irish drum, thrumming a warning for all to beware. Our black veils lay majestically across our white habits. Winnie softly reached for her veil and I closed my eyes. I just simply could not watch her put that on her head.

"Fiona, look what's here! Open your eyes!!"

Winnie was holding a bulging, white plastic bag with Grannie's signature written in her frail hand. She bowed before me and handed me the bag. I dreaded to see what was in it.

I stole a glance to the door, as I heard some of the nuns coming up the stairs. They needed to keep out. Grannie's bag was quite heavy, and the tie was no longer able to hold it together.

It was packed with $100 dollar bills. To absolute over-flowing. Probably a ton of $100 dollar bills.

"How did you get this, Winnie?? Tell me the truth, right this instant! They will kick us out when they see what you have had hidden here all these years. Where the hell did this come from?? Did you steal it?"

I closed my eyes and felt so rich and worldly and complete, and at the same time, I felt so guilty, so greedy, so garish. My hands were shaking like when I got my gold ring as we made Final Profession to the wheezing, old Bishop. Five years earlier I had promised God to always honor my vow of Poverty, to have treasures stored in heaven, not in Grannie's old black bag.

Grannie would always slip us a $20 and say us poor girls 'never have two nickels to rub together'. We were not supposed to have our own money, as all we had to do was to get down on our knees and ask for a toothbrush or a pair of shoes.

I could not look at Winnie. I know she had that expression she carried with her – she took it out when she figured she had out-smarted me and painted it all over her face. The Queen was in the Counting House, counting all her money.

"I thought we were supposed to turn in any money we received or earned. Our habits have no pockets, Winifred, and everything we will ever need is provided for us by the Community. This is an absolute sin and I want nothing to do with it. And I will not get you out of this. Not a chance – you are on your own, Baby!"

I expected her to start begging or whining or crying. A good pout from Winifred O'Grady could last a week if she were up for it. But now she was absolutely gloating, triumphant, at the top of her game.

"Well, Fiona, aren't you the smart one, with your Ph.D. from Notre Dame and all on scholarship like the rest of your brainy Flahertys who drink it down faster than they can make it.

"Grannie gave me the money on my word that I would not turn it in. Our uncle, Jack Gilhooly, told her she could dispense us from our vow of poverty, just this one time, because she was the oldest of our blood-relations. She said big changes were coming to the Church and nuns and, who knows, but we will need the money someday. So there"

Winnie absolutely had me. Why did Grannie trust her and not me, me with my Notre Dame Ph.D. in Social Psychology that no one knew what it meant. I got out-foxed!

While Winnie was an Earth Mother, built close to the earth, I lived in my head, rationalizing, ruminating, reflecting on all the variables, deliberating on the old paradigms, new prototypes, the stubborn archetypes under which we drew our energy. I was 10" taller than Winnie. People could not believe that we were even related.

And Uncle Jack Gilhooly, the Holy Monsignor, was not a man to be trusted. Nor was he holy. He was always doing funny stuff with money, despite being the Cardinal's topman with the finances in the Archdiocese.

He and Grannie came over from Ireland when they were just in their early 20's. Somehow, he'd always be pulling quarters out of our ears to show how magic he was. We really did not like him, because he was so scary, but we always acted politely.

After he was ordained, the Cardinal had him traipse around with him when he went to the parishes at night to confirm kids, meet with bankers and lawyers, talk with radio and tv people. He sent Jack to DePaul for his law degree.

So, with his gorgeous looks and mellow Clare accent that would flow like an eel into your ears, his uncanny sense of money and the Cardinal behind him, no one could touch Msgr. Jack Gilhooly.

Sometimes we could barely look at him. I always wondered if he had a girlfriend. Grannie would have tarred and feathered him. Not him.

I threw the money on the bed and left Winnie's room. I got in the shower and pulled my hair at the roots. Is this what you called an "existential dilemma"?

Chapter Four

Making No Small Plans

I finally got to sleep. My life was changing faster than butterflies fly. I threw on some clothes and stole up to Winnie's room. The sun was just breaking over the dark slate tiles on the college's steep roof and I knew Winnie would still be asleep.

I stood outside her door like a little mouse, afraid to snap her trap. I smelled something funny, something strange that I did not recognize, but I had a suspicion. Without a sound, I opened her door and was smacked in the face with sweet, sickly smoke.

Winnie was perched at the head of her bed, smoking, as she looked down at the dead nuns dancing and running in the cemetery. It was raining hard, but the dead nuns, oblivious of the weather, ran through it and did cartwheels over their own wet gravestones. When they looked up, Winnie would wave and some of the younger nuns would wave back.

"Winnie, what in the Name of God are you doing? What is all this crap in the air?" She was perched like the Queen of the Dead, the black Notre Dame sweat-shirt (XX large) I gave her ten years ago hung loosely from her diminished shoulders. She blew smoke at me.

"Fiona, Fiona…Grow up, will you?? It is all legal now and it helps you relax. Just ask your doctor. And for pain, Fiona."

I scratched the back of my head, like I do when I do not know what to do. My hair was always dark, very dark and I caught a reflection of myself in Winnie's mirror. For a second, I did not know who that was with streaky gray hair, brownish-gray eyes, and my slightly prominent, thin nose. I always looked serious because I was serious.

"Just tell me where you get this! Is this where Grannie's money is going? Up your nose? Winnie! Even after 54 years, they will send you packing, right on home where you belong!!"

"Gino Turelli! Gino Turelli brings it to me, Fiona! You know, I think he really likes me. Even if he just works around here in his blue uniform, he drives a silver

Mercedes and smokes Cuban cigars. His wife died 17 years ago - Kitty Kelly! You must remember her! Gino Turelli is a real gentleman, Fiona!"

"Please throw that out the window, Winnie! It is making me sick. What else does your Gino Turelli give you? The poor old widower with his silver Mercedes."

Winnie put the joint out against the cement windowsill, slipped off her bed like a little girl, discovering Christmas presents hidden under a bed. She stealthily reached under her bed to draw out another suitcase with travel stickers to Sicily, Rome, Turin, Venice, Naples.

Like an agent for the FBI, she diligently opened it and men's denim work-clothes tumbled out. Denim jeans, all sizes, all states of tear, burn, cut, rip, buttons, and no buttons.

"Gino told me I just might need these someday. They were too great to throw away. I think his kids worked here after the mother died and they wore some of these. Mother Madeleine Marie always wanted the guys to look good, slaving over us like we were little princesses."

Winnie picked up a few of the uniforms, shook them out and held it up to her. Her eyes matched the faded, blue denim almost perfectly. She looked in the mirror and gasped. Winnie liked what she saw. Whoever heard of a beautiful old lady?

***

We have money and a boatload of old jeans. Winnie is smoking pot and Gino may be looking for another wife. There is no one like our Winnie O'Grady. Suddenly I burst out laughing. Who is the good guy? Who is the bad one?

"Oh Winnie! Speaking of Gino, do you remember my first year, first grade, at St. Anthony's?? The principal told us we'd have a fire-drill that morning and we practiced the whole thing, from the sound of the bell, getting out of the school, not burning to death."

Then as I was getting my 65 little kids out of the school when that blood-curdling bell rang, Billy Blake, that crazy old drunk of a janitor, was standing by the exit door, shouting at the kids, "Get the hell out of here! Run as fast as you can, ya' little fairies!! Do you want to look like burnt toast?? Get the hell out of here!! You'll burn to a crisp!!".

I was the fool – telling them to walk nicely, do not panic, the fire chief from our village will be right there. Remember, this is only a practice. No fire, just like rehearsing for a play. I could have killed Billy Blake – he made me out to be a liar in front of my kids.

When we got back, some of the kids were crying, some laughing, boys holding themselves so they would not wet. Sweet Jesus, I put on ten years that morning.

The desire to be a nun had formed deep in my heart when I was a junior in high school. The nuns all seemed so grace-filled, holy, focused on God. Then a year as a postulant, two years as a novice, making vows and anticipating it was all going to be serene. Then Billy Blake comes into my life.

I had never anticipated fire-drills, much less fires and tragedies in Catholic schools. There has been many large fires and Lake Michigan tragedies in Chicago, but the fire at Our Lady of Angels in 1959 really hit me. The

31

thought of all those children and their parents, destroyed forever. Three nuns and 92 children lost their lives.

**

I was 21 and teaching first grade. There was a rumor among the nuns in the city that a nun saw the fire and ran around the old school looking for the principal to get permission to pull the fire alarm. To do anything out of the ordinary, like taking a phone call or going to the dentist, required permission from the superior. Common sense rarely prevailed.

In those days, the principal frequently taught one of the upper grades and was also the superior in the convent. The poor woman rarely got a rest or a chance to come out of her carefully defined roles.

Years later, my fascination with Social Psychology brought me to Notre Dame. I was quite conflicted about the nun who did not pull the alarm. Was she that brow-beaten by her vows and superiors that she was devoid of common sense? Did smoke and flames render her delirious? Was she afraid of making decisions? Was she afraid of being wrong?

There was a wonderful loophole to resolve situations such as this. It was called "presuming permission", to be used in a crisis. Or when there was no one available to grant permission.

Or was it all a lie? Did a ground swell of antipathy against Catholics, against all nuns, or her personally, making her a welcoming target for hate and anger? No one could figure out how and why the fire was allowed to roar in that old section of the city, so an iconic nun took the blame.

Maybe all the nuns were in their classrooms and no one was running around looking for the principal. It was easy to blame one of the nuns.

Chapter Five

I Will Arise and Go Now

At this time of my life, I really feel that "peace comes dropping slow" with understanding. Not knowledge, just understanding and accepting the things we cannot change.

While Winnie watches and waves to the dead nuns romping and running over their graves, I have discovered a greater wonder right in the same place.

As the 14th circle was closing at our congregation's cemetery, our former Mother General, Regina Ryan, beloved by all, was laid ever so gently in her grave. She lived to be nearly 100.

She was a beauty to behold: Tall and like a beautiful swan, bright, holy, funny, leading us ahead when half of the community left. Now I understand that us younger nuns projected onto her our broken, immature selves. We all wanted to be like Mother Regina.

Projection is something we do all the time. It is a psychological mechanism for us to deal with emotions buried within us that we do not know how to handle.

This can be negative – if I do not want to consciously acknowledge that I am lazy, I call the Irish from Cork City lazy. In a somewhat positive way, a young woman, unaware of her own strength, is marrying a man who she perceives as strong.

Apart from all the historical and political aspect of elections, it seems that millions of Americans, suffering poverty and diminishment, projected onto Donald Trump wealth and glory, aspects of themselves that they felt would be restored by the narcissism of the great brand maker.

We project onto sports figures, saints, movie stars, poets and novelists, our deepest desires for ourselves. We can understand the dreams you had as a child by looking at who was hanging on your bedroom wall.

Beautiful Mother Regina, the repository for all our needy projections, was placed in the earth reverently, like the host on the paten. In her waxy hands, she held a parchment scroll with her vows that she had kept so religiously. We all wanted to be like she was.

Another nun died and would be buried in the 14th circle, right next to Mother Regina. As the gentle humor of Our Lord would have it, the next nun was the direct opposite of Regina.

Sister Edgar Jude was short and plump, with her eyes unable to be focused, so you never knew where she was looking. She barely got out of St. Mary College up here, right next to the Motherhouse, where all the nuns and girls from the town and around were educated.

Poor Sr. Edgar Jude had horrible skin psoriasis, a body odor you would never forget. And her feet were severely pointed toward each other. Her teeth were always in poor repair.

It was so much easier for Mother Regina to negotiate the world as a nun than poor Sr. Edgar Jude. But whom did the Good Lord love the most? I think He insanely loved them both, no question about it! While they inhabited the extremes of women who were nuns, the Lord kept them both safe, protected from the harsh judgment of others.

And wasn't He always ready for a time of learning? We never would have elected Sr. Edgar Jude as our Mother General. She was destined to teach 2nd Grade all her life, in the poorest of parishes, in the worst neighborhoods.

In some of the more exclusive, wealthiest of parishes, the pastor would demand to have the most beautiful nuns to staff his school. Sr. Edgar Jude never had a chance. Nuns who had been declared "beautiful" by some arbitrary standard would subtly drop into a conversation that she had been sent to St. Brendan Parish.

As I have thought of life in such a different way and as I myself have ripened, I think Sr. Edgar Jude was a very old soul. She had no need of the accoutrements of Mother Regina. She had been around for many lifetimes. Regina was simply a new soul.

Many of the nuns have frowned upon me when I refer to reincarnation. Didn't Jesus say, "Whom do men say I am? John the Baptist? Elias? Jeremias?" I rest my case.

I have always loved the Lord with all my heart, and I love His creation, big and small, always perfect in ways that only He can see. In His loving heart, Mother Regina and Sister Edgar Jude are both loved dearly, deeply, without a single doubt. Winnie kept her sharp eyes on the both of them, grave mates in the hereafter.

Chapter Six

Blue Jean Baby

I did not see Winnie at the funeral for the elderly sister who was slowing dying for so many months. It felt like she feared to take that leap into the great Unknown. I sometimes wonder if we are the one who choose when we lift off – our biology, emotion, and spirituality all a part of that decision.

I am getting concern, as I sense Gino has been drawing closer to Winnie and farther from me. He is hanging around her all the time. I must get this settled between us: what is going on with her and Gino?

I was growing agitated with Winnie, yet I used our special code on Winnie's door, louder than was necessary, just so we would know who was there. We never went in each other's room unless we knocked. We needed to respect each other's boundaries. "Fiona, I'm coming," shouted Winnie.

On her bed were piles of plain denim in myriad shades of blue from Gino's jeans. Millions of tiny pieces of white thread were in the basket. She told me that Gino would wash them again and then put them through the mangle for us.

When I was in high school, my mother made me go down the basement and put sheets and some of the boys' clothes through the mangle. I had to use both my hands and one knee. I hated doing it, I could not make it work right, and stormed up the stairs to tell my mother I simply could not do it. She smiled at me, "Well, I guess you'll never learn how to drive." Those clothes were done in a flash.

"I just don't get it, Fiona. I know you are getting antsy like you do. You got that Gypsy Rover deep in your soul. I do know. This is where we differ the greatest – I can sit here all day with Kitty Turelli's seam-ripper and pull these jeans apart. Kitty was Gino's wife. I guess he did not have the heart to throw it out when she died, leaving him with all those boys."

Winnie had grown up in a family surrounded by her father's depression. The air was heavy, and it seemed that the floors kept sinking lower and lower with the father's blacker moods. Joy was a stranger; laughter was not welcome.

When you grow up with alcoholism, life is unpredictable. What shape is he in? How did the gravel sound in the driveway when he pulled up? I was the oldest of the six Flaherty kids and knew I had to protect everyone.

Through good therapy, I discovered that I am hyper-vigilant, on my toes at all times. He would frequently have his gun out from when he was a detective and tell us that we were going to die, our blood flowing like a mighty red river, right off to sea.

When I was 11, I had to take his gun away, make scrambled eggs for him, and stick him in bed. My mother never knew when she should not torment him, as she would yell at him when he was tight. I caught on early. So, between Winnie and me, we keep our fathers' depression and alcoholism very much alive.

"Then, Winnie, what happens with all these scraps of dirty denim? You going to make wallpaper? I think those threads are getting up your nose. You keep rubbing your freckles, Winnie!"

I smiled at Winnie. I was just finishing a wonderful book about a woman in WW II, working against the Nazis.

Set in the French couture world of high fashion, she was able to make a flowing, midnight blue evening gown out of fabric scraps. It was all done by hand, and not a stitch shown. In other words, 'do not sneer at scraps!'

Winnie put down her seam-ripper, blew her nose, and smiled at me with a considered rehearsal. She could feel the restlessness growing in me, as my foot was always tapping, my fingers rapping on a hard surface. "Fiona, do you ever feel you'd like to get active in ministry again? You're sure healthy enough."

"Winnie, what in the name of the Most Holy Lord are they going to do with two wrinkly 73–year olds? In a few years, they are going to be ministering to us.

"Cuz, are you too old to wear jeans? Just wait until you see what I can do with them! Your legs are longer than mine, so you will use more material for your habit. Just you wait, *Blue Jean Baby, Denim Daisy, painted on so tight!*"

I started to laugh. I picked up a swath of an oil-stained leg and rapped it around my head. I blessed myself, reached for a bit of palm that Winnie received on Palm

Sunday and stuck in my mouth, and within seconds, I was doing my ill-gotten ballet movements, pirouetting while Winnie smiled like a mother at me. I was spinning, whirling, twirling and so fast that I fell and cracked my head on Winnie's wooden dresser.

Winnie threw the denim and sewing materials on the floor, made me lie on her bed and got a cold washcloth for my head.

We stood and looked at each other – just a few seconds too long. We could not get too close. It was said that 'Our boundaries keep us safe.' Lordy, we had to be safe at all cost.

Winnie became serious and spoke as if she were enlightening someone with a thick skull. She is looking at herself in the mirror as she speaks.

"Fiona, despite all your smarts, are you aware that denim is now the fabric for everyone: men, women, kids, babies! Gino even wears classy jeans when he is all dressed up! All over the world, for rich or poor – some jeans sell for hundreds of dollars. Old, even antique jeans worn in the Gold Rush are up in the thousands."

43

"So..."

"I would just love to wear a habit again. I think it is the most powerful symbol of all. It tells everyone that we represent the church. It also told us that we were belonged to the church. It invited people to come up and talk with us. And for the businessmen to pay for our lunches and we would not even know until we went to pay.

"Nice big sleeves, my rosary at my fingertips, pockets deep enough for all of Grannie's money, some weed for an emergency, Patrick's old Swiss army knife. Maybe even air-line tickets, first-class," Winnie dreamed aloud.

"So, you are talking jeans and wearing the habit again? Winnie! Winnie, is that where you're going with all this?"

"Dear Mother of God, forgive us! What are you thinking about, Winnie? Are you going to be a new pioneer, like Amelia Earhart? Hillary Clinton? Nancy Pelosi? No!! Catherine McAuley!! To start another Mercy order like she did, the Little Ladies of Lower Baggott street?"

"Fiona! Just for you and me, the Gilhooly girls, too young to retire, too old to wear our original habits. Just wearing a new, powerful symbol, because the two of us are too young and energetic to be led out to pasture, just like the church."

Chapter Seven

The Blues Sisters

Winnie had not come down for breakfast. I picture my cousin blowing smoke out the window. Slowly I open her door. Winnie was sound asleep, snoring ever so softly. She was still in her clothes from yesterday. I lay the back of my hand on Winnie's forehead.

"Fiona?? What time is it? What are you doing up here?"

I hand Winnie a cup of strong tea and help her sit up. Winnie looks different, as if she had seen something strange, stranger than that strangeness she was used to seeing.

"Fiona, I sat vigil throughout the night with old Grace Donovan. Gracie was on her way into the arms of Jesus and I did not want her to be alone. Gracie was not the least bit afraid and she kept talking to her mother. The last time she saw her mother was when she left Ballinasloe to come to America to enter the convent. That entire family is all gone now."

I knew that I would never really have it over Winnie. Her heart was as big as a mountain, covered with bluebells. There was never a moment of deliberation for Winnie, as her feet were out the door before she ever knew where she was going. That was her Earth Mother energy, not hypervigilance, like me.

"It was such a time of total grace for Gracie. She was picking at her nightie, then she would look me dead in the eye and pick at her baby-blue nightie and point north and east. I would lean down and hear her whisper. 'Irrland ... Irrland'. I would ask her if she were going to Ireland and she would shake her head. She'd pick at her blue nightie and point toward Ireland."

"Winnie...Winnie, now listen carefully. You have your gifts, right from the hands of the Good Lord, Winnie. That is why you were with Gracie right at the end. You do know what she was telling you, Winnie. It was for you to share with me."

Winnie's big, mother-smile broke across her plump, freckly face. A flash of sunlight broke through Winnie's window and she said under her breath, "I just thought I dreamed it all." Winnie handed her empty cup to me, lay

47

back upon her fluffy pillow, and motioned for me to sit down on the edge of her bed.

"Promise you won't get mad at me, Fiona?" I nodded my head, crossed my heart, and held Winnie's hand. "If this sounds crazy, Fiona, blame it on Gracie. I was with her right as she drew her last breath, and I saw God's Holy Angels filling Gracie's room. Her old smile would break your heart."

Winnie raised herself up on her right elbow and began to tell me that Gracie wanted us to go back to Ireland in our new habits, blue made from Gino's denim blue jeans. Grannie gave us the money, we know how to pray, if we get into trouble there is always the memory of Msgr. Jack Gilhooly.

"We are not to sneak out in the black of night, but to tell the superiors what we have been called to do. We will need their prayers, but no permissions from the bishop or cardinals. The rest of the nuns do not need to know until we are gone. Gracie in heaven and Gino on earth will be our special angels.

We both knew how the church has gone to hell over in Ireland. The little old churches used to be bursting at the seams with the Faithful, now they are as hollowed out as a deserted farmhouse. There are no nuns or priests anymore to fill the streets in every town and village.

The last time we were in Ireland, in 2017, we went up to Kildare to make a visit at the Shrine of St. Brigid. We went into a parking lot and a young Garda was directing traffic. We asked him where to find Brigid's shrine and he did not know who she was or what we were talking about. I felt a stab in the heart.

A dear friend of mine was cycling with a pal from Limerick. They were far in the country and stopped to make a visit to a small chapel tucked into the mountains. An old lady, wrapped in her tattered brown shawl, was kneeling on the stony floor in front of the communion railing.

They went to see if she needed any help. She told the boys to run and get the priest. A bit of bread from the Holy Eucharist had fallen on the floor during communion. Only a priest could touch the Blessed Sacrament in those days, and she did not want anyone to step on it.

It was the deep, fervent faith of the Irish people that burned in every heart. That very faith sent thousands and thousands of missionaries all over the world. The Irish carried their faith to America, Australia, New Zealand, as well as Scotland and Wales. It felt rather discordant to be returning to Ireland with the faith.

Winnie said that one of the younger nuns is in the hospital. She lived alone and we are to go and take care of her place. She has a sewing machine and we can make our clothes over there without disturbing the other nuns. The first thing we are to do, in the Spirit of Obedience, is to talk with Mother Carmelita for her permission and her wisdom.

"Winnie, what about veils or hats? It is raining all the time over there, and if we have habits, should we have veils? You bump into everyone when you're carrying an umbrella"

Winnie laughed, jumped out of bed, and drew a white *bonnie* fisherman's hat out of her drawer, rolled up and tucked between her underwear. It was nice and soft, so easy to roll up, stretch out, throw into the washing machine, or even wash by hand.

So often I feel like I have 20 wild horses galloping in my chest. They make me restless, uneasy, distracted. I just want to get away, like I did as a kid when my father, Peter Flaherty, was on a tear and he would be up for killing all of us, all eight, including my mother.

I hope he will not follow me back home to County Clare, where the Flahertys once lived and breathed and had their being. Still, we are now returning, to bring a spot of grace to that forsaken land.

Chapter Eight

The Diaspora

Things began to fall into place for us. On a very strange, but delightful level, Winnie seemed to have come into her own. After praying intensely and working out our plans as best we could, we did not get on our knees, but simply sat down with Mother Carmelita. We were collaborating.

We wanted to go to Ireland to help them in healing the bizarre history of the Irish people with the church. They were under the heel of England for 800 years; since 1922, the Catholic Church had a noose around the Irish neck.

Our cousin Jeannie has gone to daily Mass since 6th grade. Now she is in her early 80's. She went home to the Gilhoolys up in the Burren last summer and the churches were empty. We cannot get her to stop talking about it.

In 1966, when Uncle Jack Gilhooly sent all of us over to Ireland for the first time, we could not get down the sidewalk with the number of priests and nuns clogging the paths. Blue, brown, white, gray, black, black, black. All the colors of the church's rainbows. The rains of change came and obscured the rainbow forever.

But, if I am honest, it is the same here. Nuns in various habits would be floating around the Catholic Schools in the years up to the 70's here. We have disappeared.

"I'm hiding, I'm hiding, and no one knows where..." It is unsettling to realize that within the church, we were the most visible, iconic symbol for decades, then we went disappeared.

After Mass one Sunday in May, right before we got out of our long, white habits, an old lady grabbed my hand and whispered in a throaty voice, "Sister, don't throw away your habits. We need you to stay right the way you are." I told her that our habits were on their way out. I felt like a traitor, yet eager for the new church.

A friend of mine, Barbara, was told by her mother, "All the trouble started when you took off your veils." Her mother would not have had three grandchildren if Barb had not taken off her veil. Even those of us who stayed, we loved having the wind in our hair and the sun on our fading roots.

While this may sound Native American, I know that there has been tremendous *Soul Loss* in the comings and goings between here and there. The primary belief is that we exist within our souls, we do not contain our souls within us, like a little tabernacle in our hearts. Our souls encompass us, bigger than our skin.

When we are about to experience danger, we leave part of our souls in a safe place until we can return and *Retrieve our Souls*. Not me, singular, but we, back as many generations that there were.

How many millions of us Irish Americans thirst to go to Ireland and when we first step onto the land, we begin to scoop up the parts of our soul that our ancestors had left.

I think that we Americans search wildly for the exact spot the 'old folks' were from. That is the very spot our great, great grandparents left our souls, just waiting for their 3rd, 4th, 5th generation of descendants to return home. Still, if we are lucky, someone will take us in their arms and say, "Welcome home, Fiona!"

Jesus said, "What does it profit a man who gains the whole world but loses his soul." If we lose something, we try to retrieve it. I have often thought that the loss of the souls of our tribe has resulted in the horrible black depression and suicides, the drinking and drugging of so many of our people.

Sure, we may not know this in our minds, but in the contours of our souls, there is no room for doubt. Wouldn't it be interesting to go to a treatment center, read the charts, and find out how much soul-loss each one has? Perhaps the time and quality of recovery is commensurate with the loss of soul. Perhaps those who never recover have suffered immeasurable soul loss.

Winnie is at her knocking again. "Come right in, Winifred. What took you so long?"

"Take off your clothes, like a good nun. That is right. Now climb into your new habit."

I stood beside Winnie with my eyes open. She would not even let me see the denim habits she had been working on until we had talked to Mother Carmelita. My heart was racing so fast, I thought it would fly out of my chest.

I threw my arms around Winnie's plump neck and shoulders and tried to breathe. Not only were our new habits gorgeous, they were exquisite. Winnie plopped the bonnie white fisherwomen's hat on my gray hair. I took it off to see what she had sown on it.

I squinted. I rubbed my eyes. Winnie had sewn the symbol of the Claddagh ring, but with the Sacred Heart of Jesus held by two hands. Now there would be no doubt what us "Yanks" were about: "We were on a mission from God", as John Belushi shouted. No more hanging over the rocks to kiss the Blarney Stone.

I looked up at my magnificent cousin with her Claddagh cap hanging over one eye. I was so proud of her and all that treasure buried deep within.

"It's all so iconic, Winnie!"

"Just shove that 'iconic' stuff of yours. Listen, Fiona, everyone knows these: denim nuns' habits, fishermen caps, Claddagh rings, white gym shoes. That is half the battle. There's no doubt now what we are about. Try not to act so superior in your head and language!"

***

There was a knock on the door. Winnie and Fiona, all dolled up in their blue jean habits and white fisherwoman caps, stared at each other, eyes open in deathly fright.

"Fiona! Winnie O!! Just please open your door. It's just me, Mother Carmelita."

"Oh, just look at the two of you! Msgr. Gilhooly would have a good laugh for himself. Well, enough about him. I want you both to see Dr. LaSpina for a good check-up, Dr. Russell for your teeth, and here are your tickets from O'Hare into Shannon, next Monday, the Feast of the Immaculate Heart of Mary.

"Next Sunday, after Mass, all the sisters will have a wonderful party to send you off to Ireland. If any of them want to give you money, please take it.

"There will be no more sending you out in the black of night, as we used to do when we were ashamed of people leaving. Then all we would find was an empty bed. You are still ours.

57

"We're so proud of you both, and I know Jack would be, too. You are going to need all of us behind you, to keep you safe, to help you meet the right people, and to keep the blessings flowing."

***

Mother Carmelite had made the appointments for us, so early the following morning, off we trudged downtown to meet with the doctors. In the middle of nowhere, Winnie stopped. A few drops of rain were washing the fat sycamore leaves above us.

"Winnie, don't start pulling that stuff now! All the doors are opening for us, and you are doing that old balky donkey stuff that all the O'Gradys do. Please don't bring that bad juju on us!"

Winnie's arms were folded, eyes down and she would not have budged an inch. Tears were joining the rain drops down her freckled cheeks.

"Fiona, I haven't been to a doctor since I was 22 and stationed at St. Martins."

"I absolutely do not believe that, Winnie."

"I just can't do it again, Fiona. Please believe me."

"Well, Winnie, I think I have a right to know. What happens if you have a heart attack up in Galway or find a lump in Dungarven? You want me to call the priest instead?"

"Ok, OK, Fiona. Do you remember when Mother Ignatius sent out that letter to all the nuns that we had to have a pap smear? Some nun got cancer in her insides and the doctor was upset that she never had any women's tests. Do you remember?"

I thought Winnie was going to tell me she had ovarian cancer or something with her bladder. I never knew where she was going.

"Fiona. I went to Dr. Quinn. I had all his kids in school. Smart kids. And it was raining that day, too!"

I was waiting. The rain was kicking up at bit, but I was not going to move. You had to strike when the iron was hot, and poor Winnie was steaming at the ears. I did not want to hear about the Quinn kids at St. Martin School in Aurora.

"So, his nurse takes me into the examining room, and I have to take off all my clothes, rosary and all. Then hop up on the examining table. Sweet Jesus! He feels my boobs, then sticks this big, cold steel machine up my front.

"Thank God the nurse was right beside me, her hands on my shoulder. Then, God forgive him, he put on some gloves and stuck his finger up my ass! UP MY ASS, Fiona!

"Then I clamped down so hard he couldn't get his finger out. He was feeling around like I was pregnant. They kept saying, "Now Sister, just relax, Sister, just relax…We're almost finished, and you've done a good job. Just, please relax, Sister."

I held poor Winnie, rain, and all. Poor, dear Winnie. We will all die virgins, never touched, all in the spirit of Chastity, but the more of Obedience.

"Did I lose my virginity, Fiona? Did I lose it?"

Chapter Nine

Windows with Stained Glass

Willie told me she would stop smoking if I stopped drinking. I have been dying for a drink as the steward rattled her cart of Irish whiskeys and soda up and down the aisle. Winnie knew I wanted a drink, but her nice, sharp elbow made me remember my promise.

When the cabin was pitch dark, we stole into the bathrooms and changed into our new, blue denim habits. On our backs were twenty years of denim work clothes, scrubbed, dismantled, ironed, and matched with a complementary tone of blue. Blue is not blue, but turquoise, baby blue, navy, pale, slate, Cape Cod, even the breathless blue of angels' eyes.

They felt stiff, ironed to a crisp. I thought they would actually break in two, or a long sleeve would snap off. If I were absolutely honest, I would say it was delightful being back in a habit. Habits are iconic symbols of commitment to God, the church and personal holiness.

In his book, *The Nun in the World,* Cardinal Suenens invites religious women to get out in the world, dress like a modern woman in tasteful, simple, non-attention-getting garb. In1963, he said we were an *Anachronism,* trying to serve 20th century society, but dressing and acting like women from the 18th or 19th centuries. Were we obsolete?

The cover of his book has roughly 25 nuns, dressed in traditional habits, from black veils, to white wimples and gussets, to sturdy, thick unfeminine black shoes. None of their feet show in the picture. Our habits were not comfortable and basically hurt as they dug into our heads, scratched our backs, hurt our feet.

Our acrylic tops and spandex bottoms were stuffed back into our duffle bags. No veils, but our floppy white hats were just the touch we needed. A simple cover for our heads, a symbol of virginity. But who would know? Who would care? We do.

So here we were, dressed in our patchwork quilts of denim blue and floppy white fisherwomen hats with $300,000 from Grannie. So, who is not conflicted these days? In the 'olden days' when we dressed the part, people would either greet us respectfully or with hostility. We really deserved neither. We were both anxious to see how our blue-jean habits would be received in Ireland.

The pale sun had just broken over the Kerry green mountains and hit me in the eye as we were making our way back to earth.

I did not know how we were going to get up to Corofin, but I had an over-whelming sense that I was no longer in charge. Responsible but not in charge – how could that be???

The first time we had come over here, the people were jumping in the aisles and singing Danny Boy at the top of their voices as we landed. Now everyone was asleep. That was in 1966 and now it was 2015, fifty years later. I always thought that Ireland, like the church, would never change. How wrong I was!

As we got ready to deplane, people were pointing and staring at us. Where did we come from?? Blue habits made out of jeans?? They can see our hair!! Old ladies do not wear jeans!

The officials sitting on the other side of the sliding doors opened their eyes, straightened their caps, and motioned us through, at the head of the line. I have forgotten the way we used to be treated – now we were nuns again, dressed like religious women.

I never thought I would say this, but maybe Cardinal Suenens was wrong and the earth needs a visible, iconic sign of the Love and Mercy of the Good Lord. Did we 'throw the baby out with the bath'?

Some accused us of hypocrisy; we accused ourselves. Did our spirit match our deeper selves? We were effected by all the turmoil of the 60's as much as everyone else.

Religious life for women had been regulated by the men of the church in 1917, men whose fantasies of religious women became institutionalized into our rules, our customs, and our attitudes. The public responded in kind. But who wants to be an anachronism?

***

We looked around, no longer accustomed to people treating us this way. A young man picked up our simple duffle bags and we made our way through throngs of people waiting for returning family and friends.

There was no one there for us. Winnie and I were on our own, with Grannie's money, the nuns' prayers, and our sharp wits. Then all of a sudden, Winnie was gone. Where was she? Probably in the bathroom or getting some coffee?

Oh, Lordy! There she was with Gino and another tall man who looked like an Irish farmer. I was mad at her but so happy to see Gino. I do not know who the other one was. Gino gave me a big hug and introduced me to the farmer.

"Fiona, here's Garrett Kelly, my Kitty Kelly's brother, just home from Africa. Garrett is my brother-in-law and I don't know how I would have raised our seven sons without him.

Garrett shook my hand and welcomed me home. Those were the sweetest words I longed to hear. Our anxieties and doubts melted away.

65

"Sister, I've never seen a habit like yours in all my days. It really makes a statement: a hip nun from the States to fix the wayward Irish."

"Mr. Kelly, I'm about as hip as a cold pot of tea with no sugar. And I have no idea about the church in Ireland"

"That is not what I hear from Gino, Sister. I hear that you and Winnie have really pulled off a great coup, coming over here in your jeans, made up like habits, with a suitcase full of pound notes...I mean dollars".

"Where's your farm, Mr. Kelly?"

Garrett looked down at Gino and raised his pale eyebrows. Gino gave a light punch to his elbow, nodding his head.

"Fiona, I'm a priest, back from 43 years in Kenya. The Bishop called me home, but I do not belong here. Gino knows how I feel. The people here hate the church so much that I can't even wear my Roman collar out on the street."

"Yeah, Winnie, they throw beer cans at him and spit right in front of him. I have been with him when that

66

happens. I think he should go back to Kenya where the folks love him, and he can say Mass in peace. There's too much money over here and the rest of the sexual stuff with hundreds of priests and kids."

I felt light-headed. My Irish farmer was really Father Garrett Kelly. I had no idea how much the people hated the church and were abusing the priests. Sweet Jesus, what did we get ourselves into?

They knew we were going up to Corofin, but it was getting too late and we all needed some sleep. Winnie and I were dropped off in Limerick to Mrs. White's on O'Curry Street. Garrett and Gino   met us the following afternoon.

Mrs. White did not make eye-conduct with Garrett when she found out that he was a priest. Chilly Mrs. White was glad to see us go. She could not put us all together and I was determined not to draw her a picture. She could ask me if it were that important to her.

We took the old way up to Ennis, the biggest town in Co. Clare. When we got to Newmarket on Fergus, there was a huge black and white sign over the door to the meat market: *Plunkett.* I knew Grannie was looking down on us.

67

Then through Clare Castle and up to the ancient town of Ennis. We drove right up to the door of Temple Gate Hotel, emblazoned in thick, gold letters. A doorman greeted us and unctuously directed us to the dining room. Garrett had told us that Temple Gate was formerly a Mercy convent and girls' school.

The kitchen was off somewhere, but the bar took up what had been the nave of the large chapel and the raised floor of the altar was now filled with a young, very loud band, towering over the entire dining room.

I looked at the stained-glass windows, looking for Our Lady and Jesus. Instead were windows stained with honorifics to: Harp Lager, Guinness Black Lager, Murphy's Irish Red, O'Hara's Irish Stout, Smithwick's Irish Ale, Kilkenny's Irish Cream Ale.

Couples were fusing into each other in the tables by the windows, a mother was changing her baby's nappy right behind us, a very old man was rocking himself to sleep at the far end of the bar, and three priests or bishops with red braid on their suits were drinking their whiskey straight.

I never really knew what blasphemy was, but I know a sacrilege when I see it. How they must hate the church! My mind turned to all those very young nuns, having left home to care for God's children, rising right at the crack of dawn, up kneeling in the cold, stony chapel, begging the blessing of Almighty God on their people.

I thought of the millions of rosaries said by the old nuns, their knees throbbing, their fingers aching with arthritis. The host, Jesus Himself, lifted up right where the drummer was slopping his Guinness all over himself. A young boy, rubbing himself to the tune of "Come Down the Mountain, Katy Daley".

I looked at Winnie. She was sipping a glass of white wine, looking down at her hands. Garrett looked uncomfortable and Gino was trying to make everyone happy, taking responsibility for everyone's feelings.

Winnie motioned for Gino to come out into the vestibule with her. I knew what she was saying. Winnie returned to the table and soon Gino came in with a tall man, wearing a studied frown. He was clearly in charge. As they had recently opened, to give the American nuns a bad

69

taste would put the *kibosh,* the curse. on Temple Gate forever.

He invited us to go back with him to his office. Winnie and I were mirroring his frown, disturbed at the loss and the intense shaming of the Mercy nuns, at the hatred for all that they had ever stood for. We were not Mercy nuns, but the Mercy nuns were our sisters.

If Uncle Jack Gilhooly had been with us, he would have chased these money-changers out of Temple Gate Hotel, just like Jesus did 2,000 years ago, shouting, *"My house shall be called the house of prayer, but ye have made it a den of thieves".*

A year later, I was in the vicinity and went back to Temple Gate. The bar and restaurant had been moved to a less convenient place. The windows were of plain glass. Good work!

Perhaps Mother Catherine McCauley who had founded the Mercy nuns up in Dublin, sent her spirit self to thank us.

Chapter Ten

Alive and Vibrant

Winnie and Gino went for the car, while Garrett and I walked down the street to find a Fish and Chip Shop. We had to settle down and forget the obscenity playing out at the Mercy convent.

"So, you two have come over to poor, old Ireland to convert the natives?", said Garrett, scanning up and down O'Connell Street for food.

"Garrett, don't be so harsh on your own people," I snapped, "we felt a push by the Holy Spirit to come back where our people are from and see if we can do a bit of healing where the church galumphed all over your necks. That's all!"

We stood shoulder to shoulder on the corner by the newsstand, watching for the car. Garrett was like no other priest I had ever met – dressed like any other man, and a purity shone on his face and his blue eyes twinkled, despite the deep pain that squeezed his heart.

"Fiona, the church in the U.S. is okay, the church here in Ireland is dead, but the church in Kenya is alive and vibrant. I wish you'd come back with me and see Jesus among the folks in Kenya."

Garrett had told us that he could not wear his collar on the streets of Ireland. Even if he were met with total silence, the looks from the people, over the years so downtrodden by the priests and nuns, the bishops and cardinals, would slay him on the spot.

Here in the land of his birth, where he was raised, educated, and called to the priesthood, Garrett Kelly was an outcast. Sometimes I felt like he would slip out of his skin and slide into the White-Crested Turaco, the strong magnificent royal blue plant-eater that flies in the thick forests of Africa.

I know how much he yearned to return to his real people, the folks from the hills of Kenya where our coffee and tea grows, a place the size of Texas with nearly twice as many people. The people there are hungry for the Word of God and Garrett could provide this for them.

Gino and Winnie approached and Garrett went for their fish and chips, the strong, familiar smell of salt and vinegar, leaking through the newspaper wrap, was perfect. We forgot Temple Gate for now.

As we finished our lovely dinner, Gino said that they were going right out to Corafin where the old Gilhooly home still stood. It was a stone's throw from Ennis, smack in the middle of the Burren.

**

Our cottage was near the small lake where the graceful white swans slept under the cool branches of the weeping willow trees. When the Gilhoolys brought twins or triplets into the world, Grampa Gilhooly and his sons added on more rooms. The place had a life of its own.

Gino had stocked the larder full of food for us and the walls had been repainted white. The plumbing in the kitchen and small bathroom was new, and in the open barn next to the house sat a second-hand red Fiat, filled with petrol.

After a nice cup of tea, we fell into bed, Winnie and I together in the biggest room and Garrett and Gino, the brothers-in-law, in the two smaller bedrooms on the other side of the house. We had the windows open, the doors locked. We slept in the sweet, fresh air like babies.

In the still of the night, I heard Gino scream, "Ah!! *Mi gonadi, mi gonadi!! Mi rocce, mi rocce!!!*" Winnie and I ran to the other side of the cabin and tried to get into Gino's room. Garrett stood before it, not allowing us entrance.

"Fiona, Winnie, this is a little embarrassing, but Gino was dreaming he was back in Wisconsin. A cow stuck her head in through the open window on top of him and he was afraid she was eating his willy, that's all!"

Winnie and I turned to go back to our rooms and we heard, "Oh, *Deus meus!, mi gonadi!, mi rocce!, mi rocce!!*"

Chapter Eleven

The Wily Bishop

Gino held the map up toward the light streaming in through the window. He squinted as he tried to follow a path through the various shaded counties, bordered by thin lines of black rivers, mountains, and forests. His elbow landed in the richly buttered dark toast, spilling a thin China cup of black coffee onto his clean khaki pants.

"Where are you going, Gino?" queried Winnie.

"Just time to get away from these Shanty Irish, these 'chicken pluckers' from Clare," he snapped, blotting his pants and table with a rag from the kitchen.

Winnie and I, having spent our time getting in touch with other nuns in the area, were unaware of their leaving so soon.

Gino was planning to accompany Garrett down to Kenya, his chance to see where Garrett lived. He was getting depressed being back around here, with few family and no work for him to do.

"So, Girls, we're going into Galway to see the bishop. You ought to come along, introduce yourselves to His Majesty, we will grab some lunch and I know Garrett will want to pop into Kenny's Books and see the old lady."

Driving to Galway, Garrett absorbed as much of the Burren as he could in the short time left in Corofin. The Burren is unique, as it is formed from sheets of limestone and sandstone that cut across the South Sound of Galway Bay to the Aran Islands. The 1934 film, *The Man of Aran,* is a story illustrating the formidable task of getting anything to grow in the harsh limestone and sandstone soil.

As the jet stream snakes north along the east coast of the Americas and crosses the Atlantic, positioning itself to come to land along the coast of Clare, it carries with it seeds, pods and traces of various vegetation from the south.

These seedlings are deposited within the miniscule cracks and corners of limestone in the Burren. I always felt they were so tenacious, with their long, hearty journey in the crashing water, then tucked under the large, flat rocks until it was warm enough to bloom.

Tourists and botanists from all over the world come to the Burren to study the various specimens trapped in the stony surface. Like scholars to a palimpsest.

I told Garrett that we would rather wait in the vestibule and then see the Bishop when he was finished. Bishop Jerry Muldoon and Garrett had studied for the priesthood together and had been ordained together by Bishop Michael Browne.

**

Bishop Browne was an imperialistic prelate, teaching Pope John XXIII to speak English with an Irish accent. As there was no imposing cathedral for the illustrious Bishop Browne, he finagled the city of Galway to turn over the ancient prison for his new cathedral.

An Irish cabinet minister described Bishop Browne as having "a soft, round baby face with shimmering clean, cornflower-blue eyes, but his mouth was small and mean." His booming voice shattered the streets and lanes, the crooked boreens and by-ways of Galway when he was giving a sermon.

Garrett had left the door to the bishop's office slightly ajar so that Gino could join them after he had parked. Garrett had been pleading his case to return to Kenya. Bishop Muldoon was silent. Garrett spoke in a hushed, sacramental tone.

"Jerry, I know this is what I must do. It is my Covenant with the Lord, with the coal-black people of the land who suffer a thousand famines each day - they are hungry, poor, unwell, unschooled, unfocused – but they have the strength of tigers, the flight of hawks and eagles, the wisdom of their fathers, the spirit of their mothers to spring tea from the stony mountains, and the power to understand with their hearts, not with their heads."

"Garrett, I need you here in Galway, but it is wrong for me to block the Holy Spirit, the very Breath of God, in your life. You have my blessing, dear pal of mine."

Just then Gino knocked on the door and entered the small office. Garrett brought us in to meet the bishop.

"Jerry, these American nuns are here to do the work that is not mine to do. Women are perfect for the 'heavy lifting'.

Garrett introduced us to the bishop, but his spirit had already left, back home to Kenya. He stood, swirling the remnants of his tea in the thin, china cup. M.B. was embossed in deep purple on the side. Michael Browne was not easily dismissed.

Chapter Twelve

The Deadly Archer

Winnie and I shook hands with the bishop. Garrett looked proud of us, two Yanks in blue-jean habits, come to do missionary work in the Land of Saints and Scholars.

As Gino and Garrett turned toward the door, Bishop Muldoon knelt beside his desk, his red flannel shirt disheveled and his jeans wearing thin.

Garrett moved toward him quickly, put his hands on the bishop's head, and began to bless him in Irish. Tears ran down our cheeks, as Garrett helped his friend to his feet and they stood, holding each other.

I was embarrassed. Should this tender moment be seen by us? They were brothers, and even more, as they shared a love of the church and the people that is rarely seen anymore. There was something else, but I had not words for it.

As Mother Carmelita had done for Winnie and me, the bishop handed Garrett two tickets for Nairobi, leaving for London in a week's time. Garrett had not expected that gift. Gino was confused, as he did not expect the Bishop to pay for his ticket.

The Bishop looked at us with nothing to drink, walked quickly into the small kitchen and brought us out a tray with cups of strong Kenyan black tea, sugar, and milk. He leaned on top of his desk as we slid back in our chairs.

Jerry Muldoon asked us how we were getting started and offered his help. The both of us looked at him, speaking a language we did not understand. He studied our faces.

"Maybe this is not the right place to brain-storm over this. You know, my offices and the cathedral were the Old Galway prison. Bishop Browne did it over so it could have a better use. I think tormented prisoners and ghosts walk around these rooms, especially Eamonn Casey who followed Michael Browne.

"Eamonn Casey was a good man who did more harm to the church than Cromwell and all their kings and queens in 800 years. England strangled us and we did nothing but flourish. Eamonn was a popular, great bishop

81

here and in England, yet he destroyed centuries of Catholicism in the blink of an eye."

Jerry brought us back in time, "Eamonn was the bishop of Galway. He was involved with an American woman, Annie Murphy, and they had a child. Eamonn would have nothing to do with his son, except that he paid his expenses.

Winnie knew that I was fading, as my mind was rolling to an old Phil Donahue Show, split screen. On one side was Eamonn Casey, arms outstretched, shouting; on the other half, Peter Murphy, his son, arms outstretched, shouting, looking for his father. This broke the camel's back."

Winnie nudged me with her elbow. I was afraid that she would start to look for a camel. She was here, totally at attention, the past and future having little space in her sights. It was scary. Why were we talking about Bishop Casey and camels?

Jerry, understanding the way that Winnie experienced the world, told her that there had been a "perfect storm" brewing in Ireland for many years – the priests were without reproach and they could do whatever they wanted sexually.

Years ago his cousin, Sean Muldoon, told his mother that a priest had been "fooling around" with him and his mother slapped him across the face, 'talking about a priest that way'. Sean died of advanced alcoholism when he was 42, up with the nuns in Kildare.

There were many reports done that revealed that certain priests and brothers had hurt thousands of children, both boys and girls. They beat and raped them, and no law could touch them because they were priests, working for the church.

The nuns ran laundries that kept young, unwed mothers prisoners for life, working in institutional laundries, and they could not be with their own children. Many of these babies were sold by the bishops to wealthy American couples looking for a sweet 'Irish baby'. Sometimes these girls got pregnant by their own fathers or by a parish priest.

Jerry went to get more tea from the scullery kitchen. I even thought I saw Eamonn Casey lurking behind his desk. Or Michael Browne. Winnie pressed her elbow against my arm. "You o.k., Fiona?"

"So then," Jerry continued, "Eamonn's secret comes out and people went running away from the churches as fast as they could. Why bother with all this, since we now know how they have been carrying on, the bloody hypocrites!"

"Jerry, do you think the people are going to come back? Garrett Kelly certainly does not think so. What is there for us to do, since the church has screwed up so bad?" mused Winnie. "We'll just be wasting our time, Jerry, and we're getting too old for this stuff."

Jerry sipped his tea and looked out the crack in the window. He smiled at Winnie, the saddest smile ever to cross a man's face. "We're all hurting, Winnie, down to our cores. We have been betrayed by God, by the church, and there is very little Faith left. Now we need women to heal us."

Winnie lifted her hands up, her palms empty. In the Novitiate we had been taught to surrender, and Winnie was doing that for us. I knew then that the Good Lord would send us our work. No fear of it, at all.

Chapter Thirteen

Just Blowin' in the Wind

In Galway at the Great Southern Hotel, we had an early dinner of baked salmon, mashed potatoes and 'three veg'. I could not get Eamonn Casey out of my mind. Back at Notre Dame one summer in the early 90's. there was a joke: They are passing out condoms at the Cathedral in Galway, just *'in Casey.'*

We were quiet, as we circled around Galway Bay and dropped down into the Burren, to our home in Corofin. There were few trees, but the flat limestone took on the look of small pools of still gray water. I wonder where Peter Murphy is now. Apples do not fall far from the tree, especially when your father is an Irish bishop of grand repute.

***

Damn! I hear that same whining or crying, like a hungry, wounded puppy or an abandoned baby. I hear it every night and when I go to look, the spaces are empty. Maybe the banshees from over the *Slieve Aughty Mountains* are having a good scream for themselves. Their cries portend death. It scares me.

In my thin nightie, I opened the front door and saw nothing. "Anybody there? Is anybody out here? Do you need something?"

I turned to go, and I heard, "Jes close the fuckin' door, Lady, just close it!" A baby whimpered and a mangy mutt began to cry. "Close it, Lady, close the fuckin' door so we can git to sleep! We've as much right to be here as youse, Lady."

God help us, from Eamonn Casey to strangers sleeping on the front stoop. I ran to wake Winnie as she made for the front door, like the troops landing on the Normandy beach. She flipped on the front light and whispered for them not to make a sound.

"Youse, too, close the damn door! I'll sic the mutt on ye's!"

Winnie stood with her arms akimbo, trying to make sense of the matted bunch before her. "You'll do no such thing, young lady! Stand up and let me have a good look at you."

The girl was no older than 15 or 16. Her brilliant red hair was caked against her skull. The mangy black mutt was sniffing her hair, her blankets wrapped tightly around her. Somewhere in the layers, a baby made a whimpering cry, so faint it could have been a young puffin from the cliffs.

***

"Sweet Jesus, who is in there, Love? Why are you hiding from us? Show us what you've got!"

As the girl offered a quick peak, Winnie saw a brand-new baby, just days out of her young mother, listless from the want of milk.

"Come in, come in quickly, all of ye, right now! Give me that little thing, here, give it to Winnie! Where is your mother?"

The young mother doubled over, "She died right at Christmas. The tumors was in her brain and she didn't know us and my father kicked her in the chest and she laid on the dirty floor and died, bleedin' right out of herself."

Winnie pealed the wet rags off the baby and saw the umbilical cord between her legs. She cut the cord and handed the baby girl to me and told me to clean her up. The new mother stood in a pool of blood, covering the floor in a circle beneath her feet.

"Who helped you with the baby, Love? Who delivered this little mite? Were you seen at hospital?"

"Jes meself and Blacky here. No hospital. She'd lick the stuff off from me and the baby. Blacky is a good mate!"

Earth Mother Winnie tore into Gino's room, flashed on the light, and told him to get out of bed. "Here's a girl bleeding to death in the kitchen, Gino, and you're sound asleep for all you're worth!"

Her name was Deirdre and she was going to call the baby Lily after her dead mother. Gino and Deirdre sped off to the hospital in Galway and Winnie tore my favorite white flannel nightie from Marshall Field's into diapers and little wrappings for tiny Lily.

I put my little finger in warm, sterile water, dipped it in sugar and put my finger in her tiny mouth, like I had seen my mother do.

Chapter Fourteen

Chaos in the Quiet Burren

I lay ever so still, with my old hand on Little Lily, counting her breaths against mine. At still nights such as these, I'd think of all the spores on the wind from Uruguay, Paraguay, Brazil, Namibia, Angola – swept into the jet stream funnel to get spilled on the sandstone and flagstone of our world here.

Then I would watch them hide under the massive stone flats, safe from the wind and rain until they were strong enough to survive. Then the sun warmed them up and they marched out and simply bloomed.

Lily began to fuss a bit. The door so softly opened, and a hand reached over me and lifted Little Lily off my bed. As he bundled her up, Garrett whispered to me, "Come with me."

I did not have time to put on my robe, but I bolted out of bed and into the kitchen after him. We changed her little nappies on the kitchen table. A fat white candle was all the light we needed.

Garrett picked her up, ever so gently and carried Lily to the sink. He handed the baby to me and motioned for me to hold her head near the water.

He poured a few pink eggcups of warm water over her little head, saying, *"I baptize you, Lily, in the name of the Father, of the Son, and of the Holy Spirit, Amen."*

He bent over and kissed her on her small head, took her tiny hands and kissed them and rubbed her little, pink feet. Garrett offered her to me, for my poor kisses and blessings. This ever so tiny infant looked at both of us and smiled. She was safe.

At this moment of such abounding grace, I looked down and the top of my nightie was open. My plump right breast was hanging out over the baby. I ran back for my robe and slippers.

The old turf fire was glowing. At this moment in time, a priest was going thousands of miles away and the baby girl, perhaps never going farther than Limerick, are comforting each other, flesh to flesh, breath to breath, eye to eye.

Garrett rocked her, ever so smoothly, and he hummed the old *Salve Regina* in her ear. When a priest dies, other priests gather and fill their lungs, singing to every nook and cranny of a church, from the sanctuary, over the nave, transepts, apse, and to the atrium.

Hail, Holy Queen, Mother of Mercy,

Our Life, our Sweetness, and our Hope

In the corner of the small room were large, white plastic Dunne's Store bags, filled to over-flowing. I walked over to look inside: nappies, blankets, onesies, powdered milk, teething rings, booties, more nappies, sheets, nursing bras.

"Garrett? Garrett, where did all this come from? Who paid for all of this? I don't get it."

Garrett motioned for me to lower my voice and come over to him. If I only had a camera or if I only could sketch our own Madonna, Garrett Kelly, and Little Lily.

"I just took a run up to Ennis and Dunne's Stores are open late. I told the lady what had happened here, and she hummed into the loud-speaker: *Rock-a-Bye-Baby.* I think they were closing, but the clerks came running with this stuff for Lily. I never would have known what to get for her, but they are mums and grannies, so they know."

I felt tears well up in my eyes. Here is a strange priest and nun, in the depth of night, feeding, changing, baptizing, and rocking a brand-new infant back to sleep.

I knew Deirdre was asleep in Winnie's big bed, after Gino brought her home from the hospital. After the doctors sewed her up, the good Irish nurses fed her, bathed her, and gave her new clothes – the rags were gone. Winnie had gotten in bed as soon as they left, just to warm the bed up for her, so she said.

"Who paid for all this stuff, Garrett? You don't have this kind of money, do you?"

"Shame on you for asking, Fiona. You *'don't look a gift horse in the mouth'*, hasn't anyone told you that? The poor women on the last shift at Dunne's Store paid for it and would brook no fuss out of me. I wasn't even in my clericals,"

"Maybe if you were, they wouldn't have given you one cent. All people have to do is take one look at your holy face and they see a martyr being stoned to death!"

"Why are you so angry, Fiona? Get on your knees and thank the Good Lord for taking care of our new baby Lily!"

Chapter Fifteen

The Troops Have Landed

After our simple dinner of rashers and eggs, with fried potatoes and a full pot of strong, black Kenyan tea, Deirdre rocked Lily and gave her a bottle of milk. Gino and Garrett would be off in just a few days and needed to tie things up.

Like Beneto Mussellini, *El Duce,* Gino Turelli took the lead, pulling out sheets of architectural drawings, legal documents, bank statements and a small calculator.

Garrett put on his glasses, looking like a professional contractor, Gino rolled up his sleeves and Deirdre moved her chair closer to the kitchen door so she could tell what was going on.

"Winnie and Fiona, Garrett and I simply cannot walk out of here and leave you two to fend for yourselves. That night I took Deidre into the Galway hospital, the head nurse, Anne Smyth, gave me her number and told me that as soon as word gets out what you two are doing, this little Gilhooly place will be swamped.

"We have made some rough drawings of expanding this house, to accommodate the abused girls and women. Like Jerry said, you do not have to search, your work will find you."

Winnie and I looked at each other. What happened to those simple days at the motherhouse, Winnie on a joint and the dead nuns chasing each other over the gravestones? We spoke not a word, as it felt strange to have the men taking control of this work in our Gilhooly home that it had not even entered our minds,

Gino began, "You don't know much about my family, but I'm the seventh son of a seventh son, and I have seven sons: Patrick, Aiden, Liam, Kevin, Declan, Seamus and Sean. My Kitty said since the boys were getting stuck with *Turelli* as their sur-name, they would be entitled to good Irish names to be called by. I didn't fight my Kitty."

Gino showed us the plans for ten '*en suite*' rooms, planning to start with ten and see how it goes. His seven sons were arriving tomorrow morning from O'Hare and would get to work immediately.

They would have to stay here. They did not drink or smoke in honor of their poor mother, Kitty Kelly, who died when they were all so much younger. They were Garrett's nephews, part Kelly all of them, and the Kellys owned the big, whole-sale hardware building and supply warehouse in Kilrush, less than ten miles from Corofin.

The bishop, Jerry Muldoon, had his lawyers getting all the deeds, contracts and permits from the commissioners and inspectors in Ennis, thanks to the Bishop of Clare, Thomas Whalen.

Gino and Garrett Kelly beamed. Winnie and I could not even meet their eyes. Diedre and Lily knew something was up. Winnie stood up like a filly at trackside, leaning against the kitchen table, knocking her chair to the floor. The baby started to cry.

"So, where the hell are we?", Winnie shouted. "This is our family's place to live, and you're making it into a five-star hotel for your fancy bishops! All this right under our nose, like us little women could never understand all the business of the world!!"

I had never seen Winnie like this, and I was beyond furious myself! "Fiona, go and pack us up and we're out of here. Your seven sons of your seven sons of your seven sons can take care of the poor babies and their wretched mothers. We're toast!"

Deidre joined Lily in crying, screaming, "Don't leave us, just don't go, please, Winnie!"

I looked at the two of them: I was completely unprepared for such antics. "So, you guys are taking off for Kenya and leaving us with seven teen-age boys we've never laid eyes on, and the house will be filled with very young women and girls, like Diedre here, with not a pot to pee in!"

"I'll tell you right now, the days of telling women, especially us harmless nuns, what to do with our lives is long over. And Gino, don't you dare walk out of here and leave us with this mess!"

"Oh, my Sweet Jesus, - Fiona, Winnie – this was not what we meant at all, I'll stay here, every second of every day and my youngest son, Sean Turelli, will go with his Uncle Garrett to Kenya."

I never knew Gino could think on his feet that fast. Winnie had propped herself against the door jamb, her arms folded like the old mothers superior. She took little Lily out of Diedre's arms, handed her to Garrett, retreated to her room and slammed the door.

The baby screamed and he handed her to me. Garrett and Gino made for the Burren to check the weeds sneaking up with the exotic plants from the West coast of Africa.

Chapter Sixteen

The Fleet is in

The boxy red Kelly truck stood high in the drive. Garrett honked as the seven Turelli brothers tumbled out, like dice thrown with abandoned on a green craps table. Gino followed behind in our small red Fiat.

From a quick glance at all this young manhood, there were three swarthy Italians and three freckled red-heads and one with dark, swarthy skin and red, auburn hair. The smallest, perhaps the 7th son of the 7th son, Sean Turelli.

Winnie and I went out to greet them, with Deirdre and Lily tucked into the fold of the entrance, shadowed from all the boys.

"I'm very pleased to meet you, Sisters. My father has told us all about you. I'm Patrick, the oldest and I'm basically in-charge. You will not have any trouble with any of us. My dear mother Kitty Kelly would be so proud that we were able to come over to help you get started."

We shook Patrick's freckled hand and the rest of them, as Patrick introduced them. You would never have known that they had been on a plane for eight hours, then this rocky road up from Shannon Airport.

Deirdre and Lily were long gone. In a flash the boys were inside with their duffle-bags strewn across the floor of the big room. When they spied the cascading plate of ham and turkey sandwiches, they dove in before Gino and Garrett came in the door.

Winnie ran to the fridge to grab more ham and ice-tea. Liam was making faces at the hungry cow with her enormous head coming in the window. Strings of saliva drooled over Gino's pillow. Liam flipped it over so his father would not see what the cow had done.

Sandwiches were gone faster than Winnie was putting them together. Winnie grabbed Kevin and told him to take over her job. She had to sit down and rock a bit. "Where's my baby?" Winnie shouted down the hall.

Deirdre tip-toed into the kitchen with Lily on her hip. The boys stood aghast. Declan snatched a sandwich from Sean's hands. "Guys," Gino shouted over the dead silence. He pointed to his small room and threw down two, large plastic clothes baskets.

As he pointed to the white one, he said, "This is for the 'reds. The others for the 'blacks' and Sean, make up your own mind. No stinkin' shoes and socks! No filthy underwear around these ladies and a baby! Your crap goes in here! Patrick, you wash this crap first, then down the line. OK, Ladies?"

"Yes, SIR!", shouted the boys. Garrett came into the room, balancing a cardboard box on his hip. He stepped on Aiden's foot, and Aiden and his uncle got on their knees to access the damage.

Garrett grabbed a handful of black tee-shirts and threw them around the room.

Kelly's Supply for All Your Needs
78 W. O'Connell Street
Kilrush, Co. Clare, Ireland

Dirty shirts and pants hit the empty baskets; the Kelly tee-shirts went on their big boy bodies. The long red Kelly truck was emptied of tools, wood, paints, lubricants, electric cords, hoses, electric equipment, ladders of wood and aluminum, tool belts, walkie-talkies, nails and screws, plastic water pipes, hinges, and ropes.

"I need two guys to sleep out here in the barn every night. I don't want a bunch of Tinkers helping themselves to this stuff. It is just for the nuns and the hard work that is ahead for us. We just need to make it perfect so they can do the work of God. Your mama would be so proud of you all." Gino smiled to himself.

Some of the boys blessed themselves. Some looked up to the blue Irish sky with dark clouds rolling in from Galway Bay. Maybe their mother could see them now. Kevin wiped a tear from his long, dark lashes and spit on the stones.

Within two hours, the interior of the barn looked like Jack Kelly's store in Kilrush. Order, range, pricing, courtesy, assistance, 'no trouble too great for Jack Kelly'. Unbeknownst to the Turellis, the four Kelly grandsons would be out in Corofin at daybreak.

***

Sweet Jesus, this was like home and me in bed with the baby. What if I had never gone in the convent? Or what if I had left in 1969 with the rest of my friends? I would have married Jerry Bresnahan and had a slew of kids. A baby to comfort and a baby to comfort me.

I love the feel of a little house, filled to the brim with kids and old folks. Here I am, rubbing sugar and a little whiskey on Lily's gums, to numb out the pain of her cutting teeth.

I love this little bundle of life, with my old hands on her little chest, feeling it go up and down, all on its own. Just pumping the joys of life to every inch of her, our own little Lily.

Our sweet *Deirdre of the Sorrows*, God, I cannot say that out loud! Deirdre is asleep with Winnie in the big bed the old Gilhoolys slept in and made their own little babies.

***

Sweet Jesus, now what is that I hear? Motorcycles in the Burren? Now they are shouting at us. Little Lily is starting to stir now that I have her calmed down. God help us, after all that has gone on today!

Winnie storms into our room, waking Lily who starts to scream with the fear of all the noise. The motorcycles are right outside the front door, revving, gunning at us while we are sound asleep.

Winnie and I open the door and three big, hairy men are straddling their black bikes like snorting Arabian stallions, rearing to sunder the gates and smoke the hurdles. The guy in the front is bald as a baby with a black beard, like a mink stole, down to his waist.

"We want our girls back, you fuckin' whores!! Who are yez to take the flesh of our flesh, the blood of our blood? Ya ugly, poxie hookers!! Git them out here or ye'll be nothin' but shite on the road, after we finish wid ye!!"

"Just you fuckin' grow up," shouts Winnie. "You'll never touch these babies again, you big, fat bullies!"

They gun their bikes even louder as the big guy charges at Winnie. I pull her behind me and hear Lily crying and gulping air. Deirdre has her wrapped in her little soft blanket, opens the door, and goes down to greet her father. He asks her, "Where's yer fookin' pimp? Where is the poxie bastard in charge here?"

Father Garrett Kelly, in his undershorts and Kelly black tee-shirt, shouts, *"In anem De, faigh amach do chuid toineanna greagach as seo!!"*

With a shout behind him, eight Turellis, all in undershorts and black Kelly tee-shirts, fill the yard with screams, shouts of danger and threats of death. Stones fly, denting and scratching the roaring cycles.

Patrick puts his long, hairy red arm around Deirdre, Lily and Winnie and motions for me to follow, "Call the Garda before we kill these bastards," Garrett shouts to me.

The Turelli boys shove the intruders off their motorcycles, ripping mirrors and rabbit tails from the handlebars. The bald, ugly man's nose starts to squirt blood as the Gardas' sirens draw closer.

Spitting the blood out of his mouth, Deirdre's father shouts, "All you fairies, get out of my way!! And you, Big Man Pimp, your blood will flow faster than my bike kicks out of this hell-hole." They roar away from the Garda close on their tail.

***

The boys go into the barn, turn on the water and clean the dirt, sweat and blood to get ready again for bed. Garrett gathers all of us in the big room, putting Deirdre and Lily in the rocking chair. Winnie motions for them to get up, and plops herself down, then holds Deirdre who holds Lily.

Garrett asks everyone to quiet down and have a cool bottle of Ballygowan spring water. The excitement is over, and he nods to Gino, there is "nothing like a bloody faction fight to sort some people out!" The baby and Winnie are fast asleep.

Garrett asks us to close our eyes and he prays in Irish and English to forgive our enemies and to bless our work, whether physical or spiritual, and thanks his sister, Kitty Kelly, the boys' mother, for protecting us in battle.

We have quieted down. I know the Gards have taken care of the men. I am sure they know about us out here, soon to be on our own. The boys have gone back to their air mattresses and I will leave Winnie alone. I lift Lily out of Deirdre's arms.

107

Next week Garrett and Sean Turelli will leave us for Africa. Garrett seemed lost in his thoughts and already, far, far away. I stand before him with Lily and ask him what he said to those guys in Irish.

He blessed himself, closed his eyes, and said, *"In the Name of God, get your hairy arses out of here fast!"*

Chapter Seventeen

The Barber Pole

As we finished the dishes, Garrett asked me if Winnie cut hair. That had been my job since I was 12. My father insisted that our three boys have crew cuts, so they would never go bald.

By 17, all three of them were bald and they were furious with me. My father thought hair was like grass and the closer it was cut, the thicker it would grow. He never let me cut his own hair, except when he was dying.

Thinking that I would be pleased, people would give me expensive barber sheers, powder and brush, and an electric razor for gifts. Like giving me an old cow if I was a dairy farmer.

I would cut the nuns' hair and some of the guys at Notre Dame. The first time when the young postulants received the religious habit and veil, they had to get haircuts.

It was bloody awful, and I hated doing it. Beautiful, young women, giving their lives to God, walking around with a secret butch haircut.

Garrett had beautiful thick, wavy dark hair, with the white dusting him in the temples. He asked me if any of his scalp was showing. I poked him in the neck and told him not to be so vain.

After the chaos of yesterday, it was nice that they were still asleep. "They" being 11 people. Winnie was going to make a nice Irish breakfast later to send them on their way, but we just needed coffee and quiet now.

"Garrett, do you know which Turelli is going with you to Kenya? It is too bad Gino has to stay here to direct his kids – but Winnie and I are really glad. It takes a lot of energy to try to control boys."

Garrett's fingers trolled his hair, to see if I missed any spots. "Just tell me if you see my scalp showing through anywhere, Fiona."

"Don't be so vain, Father! You have your vows and your vocation, so a little scalp showing will keep you humble."

"WHERE?? Just WHERE?"

"Oh, my God, you're serious! You've still a full head of hair, Garrett, so thank the Good Lord he has spared you a shining pate for the rest of your life. Now you go off in peace, Garrett, with a full head of that great Kelly hair!"

Before we ate, Garrett said Mass at the kitchen table, using an old jelly glass for his chalice. Winnie had made the wheat bread the day before. At the kiss of peace, Garrett shook hands with all the boys and kissed both Winnie and me on the top of our heads.

Garrett and Sean Turelli's duffle bags were standing at the front door. There was a knock on the door. I opened the door to a young livery man, his curly red hair trying to behave under his illustrious black cap. "Patrick Muldoon, at your service, Ma'am"

In the drive was his midnight blue Mercedes Benz limo with the license from County Galway: Y E E C. I looked at him, bending to pick up the luggage.

"Who is YEEC?", I asked.

He frowned at my ignorance: "Your Excellency, Eamonn Casey". Poor Patrick here gets to drive Bishop

Muldoon's pals around in poor Eamonn's car, because Jerry is my brother!"

***

I walked over to the car, curious about the interior of Casey's car. A fully stocked bar, fresh newspapers, music, flowers. As Garrett and Sean walked toward the door, Deirdre screamed and tore at Garrett, her thin hands around the back of his leather belt, screaming, "No, No, No Go!" and kicking him in the ankle.

Deirdre threw the baby's blanket over Sean, knocked him down and dragged him into her room. Lily started to scream. Deirdre shouted over and over, "Don't go! Stay here with us! No leave!!"

Gino had had it! He yanked Sean up onto his feet, shook him and told him to get his pink ass in that damn car. He cried, "No, Dad, no! I can't go! Please don't make me, Dad!!

Gino looked up at his brother-in-law, "You too, Fr. Kelly, you too. Get in the damn car and be off!"

Winnie ran to hold Deirdre close to herself so she would not see them walking away.

She understood a kindred soul in this young girl, and Winnie knew that Deirdre knew what she saw. The angels do not make mistakes and Deirdre had Winnie's gift of seeing where others were blind.

Patrick held the limo's door open for Garrett and Sean, Garrett acting as if to give him a nice tip. Their flight was in two hours; Corofin was not far from Shannon, then a short trip from Shannon to Heathrow.

From London, Garrett call Gino, "Bring your son home, Gino. I cannot take him with me any longer. It does not feel right to take him where I am going. I'm going to put him right back on that Aer Lingus to Shannon." As he put down the receiver, he began humming to himself the *Salve Regina* - the Brotherhood of Priests.

Sean Turelli arrived back at Shannon as Garrett was getting on the plane for Africa. Patrick Muldoon was waiting for him with Eamonn Casey's Mercedes. They stopped for lunch at *Matt the Threshers* on the Killaloe road.

Gino had said nothing to anyone, and as Sean returned home in Corofin, everyone felt that they were seeing a ghost. Deirdre screamed when she saw him and Lily echoed her scream, sending the little cabin rocking in the wind.

Chapter Eighteen

Forever in Blue Jeans

Garrett's leaving had pulled the oxygen out of the house. The limestone out of the Burren. The waves out of the sea. I think I would hear his voice and it would be one of the Turelli or Kelly boys. I 'd get a whiff of Garrett's soap and look around for him.

Six weeks had passed since Garrett left. Sometimes it felt like years and at other times it was only yesterday. Being in the convent gives you a strange sense of time. I love Garrett with every ounce of strength I have, not romantic love, I didn't want to sleep with him. I simply loved him.

Then I'd think of Africa with Kenya off to the East and, like a big, red heart, it pulsing with Garrett's blood, his laughter and prayer, his love of his tea farm and all the folks who worked with him.

But most of all of *Michael Collins*, his magnificent old Irish wolf hound, who would have been gone years ago were it not for the wet and warmth of Kenya. Garrett named him after an Irish hero in the War of Independence with England.

I'd hear Garrett referring to his four-legged Michael Collins as a "traitor", and that he'd meet his own *Be'al na mBla'th* soon enough if he didn't mind. (That was the spot in County Cork where Michael Collins was ambushed and killed.)

The boys, with four Kelly cousins, were out with Gino planning tomorrow's work. Two extensions shot straight out from the back of the house. Five *en suite* bedrooms in each side, with bunkbeds built into the walls of each, so it would hold twenty women, with space for children.

I am glad we had the house for ourselves, to start to contain the reality that Garrett was far away. Winnie brought me a nice cup of tea and began to rock. Everything had been said, but nothing had been said.

From the first day I met him at Shannon Airport, I have been struggling within myself to figure out what made him tick. I liked him immediately, the old Irish farmer.

But here was something very different that I could not name. He was totally present, totally focused on whatever he was doing – saying mass, painting walls, feeding the baby, playing with the boys, arguing with Gino. I would love to see him with his people in Kenya.

He was fully present, and he gave of himself completely, but there was space within him where he was present to Africa at the same time, without really being a divided person. I once thought he was like a man with two families who could gracefully slide from one to the other, and he alone knowing it.

Ahhhhh! Garrett Kelly lived the Covenant. He gave every second of every day, every drop of his blood, every thought in his head, every muscle in his body, every breath he drew and every morsel he swallowed – he gave it to the Lord through his priesthood, through his manhood, through his Baptism.

Garrett had a living Covenant with the Lord to have whatever He wanted from him; the Lord would protect and provide for Garrett every day of his life. It was an intense love affair, one that few have ever experienced. It made him the man and the priest he was and always will be.

"Fiona, I think they're winding down. Have you been back to see what they have done? They remind me of the craftsmen in the Middle Ages, using each of their talents to make this dream a reality." Winnie smiled to herself, proud of the work of so many of us. Dreams come true!

Two of the boys slept in the barn each night to keep watch over the equipment and supplies. Gino had wrapped his gun in a black Kelly's Supply tee-shirt and stuck it, with a box of ammunition, behind the paint cans.

The guys on motorcycles did not show up, but we never felt that they were gone. What an ugly scene they made, them with their "hairy arses". The Garda sweep by a few times a day and remind us that they were just down the road and to call if we ever need them.

***

Winnie and I had been talking about a party since the work began. The people, official or plain, had been generous and gracious to us since Day One. In all humility, we needed to acknowledge their welcoming us and their generosity.

The date was set: May 9th at half 5, 5:30 p.m. The night before the party, I was troubled and could not get to sleep. I heard sharp, thin squeals or screams or shrieks, like an animal caught between the flagstones or in the mouths of wolves or rats. I had never heard that before.

When I was a kid, I loved to scream when I ran around the neighborhood, playing cops and robbers, or cowboys and Indians. It released all the fear that my father would kill us, as he so often promised when he was drinking. He said I sounded like the Banshees, screaming the way I did. They warned of death.

List of friends appeared and soon places like our own Temple Gate Hotel, Matt the Threshers, the Hurlers, Molly's in Killaloe, and even the Great Southern in Galway wanted to bring the food and drink.

We made our first major decision – no booze. Just tea and soft drinks and Ballygowan water, both still and sparkling. The Turelli boys had promised their mother, Kitty Kelly, before she died, that they would not drink, so they were not a problem.

Both Tommy Whalen, Bishop of Clare and Jerry Muldoon were with us. Tommy, Jerry, and Garrett had been together in the seminary up in Maynooth and at the Pontifical Irish College in Rome, where bishops were "made". Garrett hated the thought of being a bishop.

We invited the Garda in for their tea, to thank them for protecting us and the boys, as well as the neighbors. All of the Kellys, including Jack's wife, whom we had never net, came with the kids who had worked with the Turellis. The boys were first cousins.

Little Deirdre had her friends from school and girl cousins who fussed and competed for the baby. Winnie took Lily back and told the girls to go outside and play. Blacky followed without missing a step. They were seriously eying the Turelli and Kelly boys and the Kelly and Turelli boys were seriously eying them. Right in the Burren.

Before we ate, the two bishops blessed the new rooms and the original Gilhooly cabin. They used holy water from St. Bridget's Well tucked under the Cliffs of Moher. The waiters from the restaurants stayed and served the food. Lily was just six months old and did not miss a trick.

After we ate, we nestled in front of the television to watch the All-Ireland semi-finals, Sligo vs. Waterford. No one made a sound - you would think we were at Mass.

The food was wonderful, nobody was drunk, and nobody was pouting, that I noticed. I glanced over at Winnie, half-asleep in the rocking chair, with Lily on her knees. I do not remember ever feeling so content as indeed, 'God's in his heaven and all's right with the world'.

Suddenly the screen went black. The regular announcer for the National Irish Television broke into the game. He looked ashen. His voice broke: "We regret this interruption. The game has been stopped. We have a message from Archbishop John Brady of Nairobi:"

"We regret to inform you, and all the people of Ireland, both North and South, that there has been a terrible tragedy on one of our tea farms in the hills of Kenya. Fr. Garrett Kelly of Kilrush, Co. Clare, has been murdered by thieves looking to burgle his small residence.

Father Kelly was tortured for several hours and stabbed repeatedly. His dog's throat was cut from ear to ear.

The television went off. We screamed and shouted and wept and wept some more. It was the remnants of a murder scene. It was the most horrible moment of my long life. People were throwing up inside and out. Even the waiters joined us.

I went into my room, tore off my blue-denim habit and slid into my nightie. I was looking for tissues, so I put my hand into the two big pockets of my habit. I drew out a dark, curly lock of Garrett's hair that had fallen into my pocket when I cut his beautiful hair six weeks ago.

Chapter Nineteen

Another Day

It was a time of sorrow, grief, and mourning. How was it possible that someone so filled to the brim with his life force could be so totally cut down in a matter of seconds? When Garrett left, I doubted that I would see him again, but I never expected this was how it would end.

The house was quiet. The Turellis headed back to Wisconsin, but Sean stayed and is finishing up high school. He was the biggest of all of them and it is good to have him around.

Garrett so often said, "I want to live and die in Kenya." Ireland was his mother, but Kenya was his wife, his lover. He had out-grown Ireland, it fit him too tightly. He could continue to grow 'firmer, gentler, stronger' in Africa.

I did not think this until he died, but I now feel that he had a strong inkling that he would not live long. I guess I will have to wait until I age even more, then I will understand. We Irish are absolutely obsessed with dying.

Ha, I was going to say with our 'mortality', but that keeps it at a safe distance. Do we know when we come to the end of our days?

John Kennedy looked up at the skyscrapers in Dallas and said to Jackie that anyone with a rifle could simply take him out. Within minutes, Oswald ended his life.

Princess Diana wrote that she was marked for death so that Prince Charles could marry Camilla. John Lennon frequently said, "I'll be popped by a loony."

The night before Martin Luther King was murdered, he said, "I've seen the Promised Land. I may not get there with you, but I've been to the Mountain top." Jesus told his apostles, "Where I am going, you cannot come."

There was a finality to Garrett's leaving, as if he had said that where he was going, we could not come. He was not referring to Kenya.

I sensed that an essential part of Garrett had left us before he had physically gone. Now I understand why he needed to send his nephew Sean back to his father and not accompany him to Africa.

Winnie and I talked frequently about that night with so many people eating and laughing and watching the All Ireland hurling and then the announcement of his horrible death. Then we would grow morbidly quiet, and one of us would put on the kettle.

We were both tired, even exhausted. Maybe we had bitten off more than we could chew. Babies, bishops, the mysteries of the Burren. At least we had each other, but it felt like it was going to be too much. Would we have been better staying at the Motherhouse?

Winnie pulled our little Fiat right up to the door. The back of the car was filled with groceries and nappies. I called for Deirdre to come and help us. Lily would be taking her nap at this time.

***

I looked up and down the short halls, opened doors, looked in the rooms. No Deirdre. No Lily. No Blacky.

Winnie honked for me. I was concerned about the food and nappies. "Hurry, Fiona, before he kills her and the baby! I am shooting straight across to Liscannor Bay. It's where all the drugs are coming in!"

I never knew if information that Winnie protected so avidly was from her visions or if she had actually heard something, just like the rest of us. Now we have Deirdre and her visions.

She shot out onto the road before I had both feet in the car. My long rosary was dragging on the street. She jammed on the break, tapped her stubby fingers on the wheel and I opened the half-closed door, pulled in my poor rosary, kissed the crucifix, and told her, "GO"!

Out on the Bay, people were paddling out on their surfboards and then were carried in on the waves that flipped them high in the air and hurled them deep into the surf. Tourists and younger kids were on the shore in Lahinch and busses pulled up to the shops.

Winnie tore past the ugly shop selling tourist items, like Connemara this and that, and headed toward the trailers and tents. Peaking from behind a battered black van were our girls, Deirdre and Lily.

"Get in the car, Deirdre!" Winnie shouted. "Right this minute!!" She sounded like Grannie, herding us in for lunch. Deirdre, with Lily on her hip, tore around the back of the van, Winnie close on her heel.

Little raggedy kids stopped playing and watched the circus, cheering Deirdre on! Lily was laughing at the top of her lungs at Winnie run in her rippling blue habit, her rosary flying in the wind, her hand on her little white fisherman's hat.

I headed Deirdre off behind the horses, nibbling on the weeds. "Winnie is going to report you to the Irish Wayward Children Association, and you will lose your baby, Deirdre!"

This is where the drugs from the Continent were coming in and those we had encountered earlier in Corofin were the top drug-dealers for both the Republic and the North. Selling items to tourists was just a front.

They looked like the old Tinkers, now made safe by the "Travelers' Protection Agreement". I would trust a Tinker way before these drug dealers, who could be from Chicago or Madrid or the Philippines.

I looked Deirdre dead in the eye. Winnie made it back to our Fiat. I could hear her breathing hard, that great old heart beating for its life.

"You know, Deirdre, he'll start abusing your little daughter in the blink of an eye. The nurse in Galway told us that many of your bones had been broken over the years and they were never properly set. Your lovely teeth knocked out. You have scars all over your body where he put out his cigarettes. You were his ashtray. Do you want that for Lily?"

"Think about it, Deirdre. Her life is in your hands. We will drive off and go directly to the authorities. You will have your daughter taken from you."

I walked down the sandy hill and got into the car. The horses were all watching. Winnie started up the car, threw it into reverse, and before she turned the wheel, Deirdre was in the back seat with Lily.

Five years before Jimi Hendrix died, he sang, "He's not gone, he's just dead." I think Fr. Garrett Kelly had something to do with this rescue, just like the last one.

Deirdre softly pinched the back of Winnie's neck and whispered, "Thanks so much."

Chapter Twenty

Visitors Unplanned

As the four of us pulled up to our simple homestead, we saw a black Mercedes off to the side. The girls had to get in the house to change Lily. The Fiat was packed with groceries. Jerry Muldoon and a small, busy woman by his side came to our door.

He saw the bags in the back and began to load up the arms of the woman. "Fiona, come meet my sister, Anne Marie, our hard-working barrister!" By now her arms were loaded down with bags of food, so she simply waved her hand and nodded her head, as she headed back to the kitchen.

"Jerry, you never told us you had a sister. Actually, you've never told us much about yourself as it is."

"What do you want to know? I am the oldest of ten. My father bailed on us after Seamus arrived, Thank God. He was an absolute terror: *"Street angel, House devil"*, we called him."

"Same here, with Peter Flaherty, who'd get itching to use his gun on us when he had the drink taken. I would practice with our Grannie's iron skillet, swinging it at his head or plunging the butcher knife in his gut. God, I hated that man!"

"Would you have actually used it on him?"

"You bet I would! I would lie in bed and wonder if it were a sin, killing my father but actually saving all eight lives under our roof! He had to go!!"

"Well, 'Leave the dead to bury the dead and get on with the living', says Jesus. I want you to meet my little sister. She is a barrister down in Limerick and I want her to know what you are doing and check insurances, finances and where we are going. Is that ok? We've talked about it before…"

"Fine, Jerry. Are you going to say Mass for us? I think we would like it. We had to go into Liscannor and rescue our little girls from the druggies. It is hard for kids so young to have to make a choice between evil parents and good strangers."

131

Jerry made a pot of tea and all of us soon gathered for Mass at the kitchen table. What better altar? Just like the Last Supper. The Muldoons had brought our entire dinner, what the Irish call our "tea", of pork chops, 'three veg', huge potatoes already baked and kept warm by his housekeeper.

Deirdre did not take her eyes off Anne Marie who focused on Lily and her bishop brother. Winnie and Lily were half-asleep. They needed to get into bed. Anne Marie's professional eyes did not miss a thing – between, around and beside us. She was racking up questions that I hope she did not ask me.

Jerry was able to answer many of her questions. I took notes and realized that our legal and tax material had to be in good order, or we risked losing our tax exemptions. Back in the states, I had always avoided this job.

Anne Marie was particularly concerned with the status of the barn, on a choice bit of land but filled with old bed springs, half-empty paint cans, tools, ladders and so much more.

Gino told his son, Sean, to finish cleaning the barn, but he has so much schoolwork and would not know what to get rid of and what to save. He is only a kid and has been babied by his older brothers, especially as their mother was gone.

Anne Smyth, the head nurse at University Hospital, Galway, is a close friend of Anne Marie and had told her that this place will be filled-to-overflowing when we were ready. She added that we needed to have a full-time nurse on the premises so we could be properly licensed.

Jerry softly mentioned that it would be nice if we had a small chapel, maybe even using the old barn. The other part of the barn could be a large artists' studio.

We had ten new rooms, each sleeping two adults and room for children. Jerry said that the bishop of Sligo had contacted the Prior of a large seminary and monastery. Those buildings are now empty, having been built 20 years ago when the church in Ireland was booming.

They were magnificently furnished, then they emptied out when Eamonn Casey started to sow his wild oats. His escapades marked the beginning of the end of the church in Ireland. They have enough for twice what we need, and he will send them down, freshly laundered, to make up the rooms with sheets, pillows, towels and rugs.

Anne Marie, looking down at her note pad, said that we would definitely need a cook, a manager, cleaner and of course, a nurse. Deirdre had not taken her eyes off Anne Marie and it was beginning to make the barrister nervous. She would swat non-existent flies.

I just wanted to slip out of my skin – this was a job for someone half our age – we were old ladies. Maybe our community knew what they were doing when they led us out to pasture.

Where was Earth Mother Winnie when I needed her? I am going to slip out to the Aran Islands so no one can get me – the air is thinner there and I will feel like I can reach up and touch the face of God.

Chapter Twenty-One

Poetry Retrieval

We woke before Lily and Deirdre. Yesterday had been a long, hard day, and if we had not been so connected with Gino, we would never have known Garrett, the bishops, the barrister, and the drug dealers.

I have thought that it has been too easy. One of our friends, Mag Quinn said, "You know you are doing the will of God when it is easy." I do not know where she got that, but it makes sense.

"Winnie, how are you doing with this? We do not even have time to talk anymore. Where are you with our new life? Have we bitten off more than we can chew?"

"That barrister scared me. What is wrong with a plain, old solicitor?", Winnie inquired, as if I could answer her questions.

"They do the heavy lifting. It is nothing like the American system. Barristers go to trial; solicitors do the paperwork."

"Fiona, how are you doing? Do you want to stay? Do you think we are cut out for this kind of work? It sure looked different from the 3rd floor of the motherhouse, you keeping your eye on poor Sister Brigid, chasing the non-existent young nuns, and me with my joint, being entertained by the dead girls down at the cemetery."

"Don't forget Gino Turelli!"

***

"Do you remember Ursula Murphy whom I worked with at the Psychotherapy Centre in Glenview? You met her a few times. She was a victim of that Baby Export business. The nuns ran the laundries for unwed mothers, so they had a great product to export. You can only bet that the greedy Irish bishops blessed these babies going to America, and the dollars that filled their coffers."

Wealthy Americans who could not have a child, purchased an Irish baby and their mothers had no idea where they had gone. Sometimes the real mothers would go to feed their babies in the nursery before they were slaving over tablecloths and sheets from the hotels.

136

'Babies gone bye-bye, babies gone bye-bye,' Sister Lucretia would sing-song to the distraught new mothers. The babies could be dead. They did not get up and jump out of their cradles at the sound of their mothers' voices. Where were they?

The system was five tiered: 1. horrible, sinful mothers bearing their family shame, 2. untarnished babies, 3. crafty, greedy bishops, 4. compliant civil servants. 5. wealthy Americans, desperate for a child.

This created a perfect storm, amounting to over 2,000 children. Exporting them like KerryGold butter or Connemara rosaries.

Ursula Murphy had a horrible story, the crazy adopting mother locking her in the closet for days, the pompous father, defiling his daughter. They would go to their country club and leave Ursula locked in the car, sweltering in the summer, freezing in the winter.

As she got more and more educated, she developed confidence, did her research, and was able to trace her parentage, location, and dates. Her mother was a wealthy horsewoman from Mungret, never married. Ursula discovered that the manager of her estate was a younger man named Charlie Quinn, who fathered her. She pictured a small cabin on rolling green Limerick hills where her father lived.

She knocked on the door and an old lady with Ursula's blue eyes and prominent mouth answered. Ursula said, "I think Charlie Quinn is my father. You must be my aunt Mary."

The door slammed shut, shaking the doorframe and the glass windows. There was a piercing scream on the other side of the door. The old lady's shame, hidden within her four walls, was now out in the world for all to behold!

Ursula and her husband then went to the Archbishop, as she had read that her mother, Alberta Russell, had left over £ 8 million to the Archbishop. There was a note in her obituary in the Limerick Leader that she was a poet of some repute.

He could keep the money – they did not want it. Ursula was desperate to see the pages of poetry that Alberta had written and saved, so Ursula would have some contact with her mother's spirit who gave her up.

They rang the Archbishop's bell. No one came to the door. Over the indoor speaker came: "Yes! Yes! What do ye want?? Answer me right now!"

So much for the friendly, welcoming Irish. Ursula explained that she was Alberta Russell's natural daughter, given up 36 years ago. She did NOT want the money but would like her mother's poetry. She knew that the Archbishop had it, as everything went to him.

"Go away!! You'll get nothing of that wonderful woman, ye little bastard!! And ye just want her money that I'm saving for the poor of Limerick. I'm jes' the 'Good Shephard' here, Girly, so go on back from where ye come from!" slobbered the Archbishop.

Ursula and her husband left empty-handed. Here she was, the closest she had ever been to her mother, but the 'Good Shephard' was blocking her way. Ursula was so distraught she threw up on the Archbishop's black marble stairs. Her husband went looking for a hose or a bucket of water. "Just leave it. That's my thank you card to himself."

***

139

We met at Anne Marie Muldoon's office, right across from the courts. She had no time to disrobe, so we saw her in her full, legal regalia – long black robe and powdered white horse-hair wig.

Anne Marie called the archbishop's offices. A timid voice said that it was too bad, but the archbishop was indisposed. Anne Marie said he had exactly one hour to bring Alberta Russell's hand-written poetry to her secretary or they could say good-by to the money.

Deirdre did not take her eyes off Anne Marie Muldoon. She had never seen a woman with as much power and respect. The Barrister was aware of Deirdre's fascination with her and began to use it wisely.

Anne Marie asked us if we would like Chinese for lunch. She had made reservations for us in the little restaurant with the Chinese red awnings, right next to Todd's Department Store. She motioned for Deirdre to sit in her squeaky red leather chair while she readied herself to meet us for lunch.

After too many eggrolls and pork-fried rice, we got ready for our trip back to Corofin. First, we had to get back to her office to retrieve the hidden poetry. I was going to post it to Ursula Murphy as soon as I was able.

The timid associate of the Archbishop was running with flatfeet down Williams Street, his thin cassock wrapping around his ostrich legs and slowing him down. He was on the clock and eight million pounds was a lot to lose.

He shouted at Anne Marie to slow down. She told him that her instructions were to give it to her secretary, up on the sixth floor.

Lily, asleep in Deirdre's arms after bowls of rice, was dead-weight. As Deirdre moved to stand closer to Anne Marie, she stopped moving away and held her ground. "Come back with me into my office", she invited them. Deidre started for the big leather chair and Anne Marie motioned her off. No cutting in line.

Anne Marie shared with us that Deirdre had raised an interest in being a barrister. Deirdre was extremely bright, but she had missed out on her education.

Anne Marie wanted to get her tested out at the new university in Castletroy and they could go from there. Also, if she left Corofin one more time without permission, she and Lily had to leave, and every opportunity was lost on the spot. Deirdre had never been taken so seriously.

We soon headed up north to Corofin. Lily was asleep in the backseat with me. Winnie drove. I flipped open Alberta Russell's notebook. Her first entry was: *Why, oh why, did I ever let her go?*

Chapter Twenty-Two

What Goes Around

I had noticed that whenever Winnie and Deirdre were at the sink, handing over Lily, fighting over the big rocker, a most subtle current of intimacy shot through them. They would nestle closer, so subtle that it was well hidden.

They both had that crippling gift of seeing things that were hidden from the rest of us. It also made them dangerous, a gift that left them speechless. I doubt that they had articulated this between themselves, so the physical bumping did the job.

Deirdre was too immature and uneducated to approach Winnie, and Winnie had made her peace years and years ago. So here am I, getting the lay of the land between them. The therapist in me wants to sit them down and *talk* about the unmentionable. That is not my role anymore.

A floppy, fat soccer ball came flying over our stone wall. Deirdre gasped and flew down the hall to her new room and slammed her door. Winnie was rocking Lily, with both of them half-asleep. Deirdre returned in a short time.

"Did you ever play soccer, Deidre?" I inquired. She shook her head.

"Just all of a sudden, it reminded me of something...a long time ago...a couple of years ago...I don't know how that works."

"The white ball?"

"Of course, Fiona, that horrible white ball!"

"I know it really upset you, Love. Sometimes one thing reminds us of another thing and we just can't figure it out."

"How do you know that stuff?", mumbled Deirdre.

"I went to school for a long time and I learned what makes us tick inside. That is why Anne Marie wants to see if you are ready to go to school. They will find that out at the university in Castletroy."

"Winnie and I can start teaching you right here, so you'll be ready for school. We have both taught about 10,000 kids back in the States...Well, close to that number."

"I've always wanted to learn. My father said that was only for Fairies, not girls like me. I couldn't fight him. My mother, she wanted…"

Deirdre screamed at the thought of her mother and tore outside to get the ball. She kicked it back over the stone wall and hit the fat cow, shaded against the old apple tree. She jumped over the wall to console the cow.

Winnie and I both clutched our rosaries, knowing we had to keep our distance. Our tough, little girl was starting to feel her feelings, as that protective block of ice was beginning to melt. She was feeling safe here, with us. Lord, if we were back at the Motherhouse, we would miss this miracle.

Anne Marie was expected to call soon, and we would then know what was going to happen with young Deirdre. I know our lives would change greatly.

With a few light beeps of his horn, Jack Kelly pulled in at the front door. We had not seen him since Garrett's murder, and we had missed all that activity with the boys. At the same time, Sean Turelli rode his bike home from school and Deirdre returned from ministering to the cow.

Jack embraced us, hugged Deirdre, lifted Lily from Winnie's arms and shook hands with Sean. Sweet Jesus, he looked so like his cousin Garrett with the strong shoulders, the black hair and deep eyes. No tool belt.

We put the kettle on and studiously waited for it to boil. Nothing like a nice cup of tea to welcome in the evening.

"So, what's cookin', Jack? We are still mourning dear Garrett. It will go on forever and ever, won't it, Jack?", Winnie murmured, with her chin on Lily's soft hair.

"Funny, I still haven't been able to watch hurling since that night. Havin' dreams about Kenya. I'm so glad Auntie Madge is gone, so she didn't have to hear this about her dearest son Garrett," offered Jack.

Sean and Deirdre were having their tea in the kitchen. Jack walked over to look at the barn and returned to his place on the couch. He scratched his chin.

"I haven't been able to do a pick of work since Garrett. I am sitting around and I'm driving my Mrs. crazy.

146

I do not want to play or work with the grandkids, go anywhere with her, even go to Mass anymore. Part of me died in Kenya that night with Garrett."

"What's on your mind, Jack?" Winnie asked somewhat harshly. She needed people to come to the point, or she would lose interest. She started bouncing Lily on her knee and Jack got the message to hurry up. Winnie would have made a terrible therapist.

"We have to do something with this old barn. It is a firetrap for man and beast. If it goes up, all our hard work is over. No more poor girls on the road. It will all be over!"

"Sounds like a threat, Jack!" I delicately announced.

"Ah, Sweet Jesus, not at all!! I have been talking to Jerry and Tom Whalen, the three of them together up in Maynooth and Rome, as you know. Jerry mentioned making the barn into a small chapel and an art studio behind it. You've got so much unused property." Jack had obviously been thinking of this for weeks.

Sean Turelli came running into the room, with Deirdre on his heels. "Uncle Jack, I heard what you said! When do we start?" Deirdre was biting her nails and Sean

147

was tugging on his ears. Strange how we dissipate our anxieties, as I began to push back my cuticles.

I closed my eyes and saw the small oratory we used when we were in the Novitiate. That was nearly sixty years ago. I feel ashamed that neither Winnie nor I thought of it. I think that Garrett Kelly would love this, and we can dedicate that oratory to him."

Chapter Twenty-Three

An Old Monk from the Mountains

It was a still, black night in the Burren. We were about to turn off the lights, when a huge lorry came rumbling across the stony fields, enough to wake the dead.

A young giant jumped out from behind the wheel, shouting to us on the stoop, "Ladies, you lookin' fer some sheets and pillows?"

I walked out to greet him, while Winnie woke Sean and Deirdre. 'Many hands make light work', as my mother used to say. The back of the truck was loaded, stem to stern, with bed and bath supplies. Into the empty rooms they delivered them, clean and pressed, but in disarray. Tomorrow would be time to sort.

Deirdre had climbed into the back and was handing down stacks of sheets and towels. The truck was almost empty. She let out a deadly scream as a rolled-up, black, fuzzy rug moved over her foot.

Sean leapt into the truck and stepped on the tattered edge, kicking it a bit to watch it move. Deirdre moved behind him, peaking at it through her fingers in front of her eyes.

"Ye bloody buggers, leave me alone, ya' hear!!"

Slowly, the raggedy rug sat up, gasping for breath. Sean stood it up on one end. Behold! A raggedy old monk appeared, covered in dust, mold, broken threads, thin strings, tape. His glasses were askew, sleeves were torn, and his straggly beard covered his face, like an old man climbing up from his deep, cold grave in the ground. Deirdre, who had seen so much worse, started to cry.

Sean shouted at him, "What you want here, Old Man? This is private property! You're not welcome here!"

"Oh, yes I am, Son. St. Paul said not to forget to welcome strangers, 'for some have entertained angels unawares.' The Lord has sent me down here to the Burren where I have never been, and I am your guest," broadcast the tattered monk.

Winnie walked out of the house to see what all the commotion was at the back of the truck. She took one look at the mess of a man; he took one look at the nun in her blue denim habit.

"Now what are you doing down here, Father? Come out of there now and have your tea and a good night's sleep. You are riding all the way down from Sligo and you no longer a young man, Father."

"Sister, don't call me 'Father'. My name is Brendan and I am a monk from our abandoned monastery in Sligo. I've nowhere to be. And your young lad told me I am not welcome!"

Winnie braced herself on his delicate arm and smiled despite herself, "Brendan, you're home now. Your tea will be ready in a flash and you can clean yourself and get into some soft clothes. Where is that lad that brought you down here?"

Brendan stood at his full height, well over 6' and shouted, "Paul, your tea is almost ready. Tidy yourself up and it is time to eat. I don't want you driving back to Cloonacool in your worn-out state of being."

From the bathroom, Brendan threw his black habit and underwear on the floor. Winnie grabbed his mangy

151

clothes and threw then in the washer. His black habit needed mending, so she would keep it away from him until it was fixed.

Garrett Kelly had kept a large box of his clothes in the closet for his return. Winnie pulled out Garrett's pajamas and robe and slippers and laid them out on her bed, like laying the vestments out for Mass.

Paul was sitting at the table, waiting for Brendan. The fluffy potatoes were cascading out of the Delph bowl. On each plate were rashers of bacon, scrambled eggs and fried green tomatoes. Clear bottles of Ballygowan water, a round bowl of fresh butter and a fat pot of black tea sat brewing on the round table.

After the men had literally gobbled down their dinner and began on their tea and raisin-bread cake, Brendan stretched his long arms, like a pelican on the cliffs, claiming his new territory. Paul held his plate up, wanting more cake.

Winnie and I sat at the table with Paul and Brendan, wondering who they were and how they came into our lives. They felt so like each other. Perhaps that is what the

Sligo men were like, as we had never met anyone from Co. Sligo.

***

Brendan, clean and beautiful, ready for bed, began his story. The monks had built a large monastery to accompany the large group of young men who entered the order every year.

Eamonn Casey's sad and wild tale came out just as the last brick was laid. The young men found something else to do, besides becoming monks. It was the beginning of the end of the institutional church in Ireland. The new monastery lay empty.

No new, young faces appeared, and, like clockwork, the old monks breathed their last breaths and were carried to their new resting places in the old cemetery beside the new monastery.

This had happened to the church all over Ireland and in many such places in the States. The Twin Towers came down in minutes, yet it took many months, many deaths, much sweat, and labor to right that bruised land.

There is no preparation for the unexpected – only clean-up, grieve, and rebuild.

I asked Brendan if he were a priest. He placed his china cup deliberately in his saucer, reverently nodded his head, and told us that he had been a priest for nearly fifty years. Much of the time he was studying the Desert Fathers in Syria and Egypt, writing and teaching in seminaries and colleges in the States and Europe.

A chill ran up and down my spine as I looked at Garrett's burgundy robe on Brendan. Paul, the other Sligo man at our table, looked into his teacup, his fat fingers about to crush the fine handle. Crumbs from the raisin cake laced his red beard.

Winnie and I were hypnotized at this man in Garrett Kelly's clothes, a man of God who had spent much of his life in scholarship.

Brendan told us that the new monastery was completely empty. He was unwilling to join another group of monks; it felt to him that he would be adopted at the age of 73, so he hid out in the new building, like a king with the castle all to himself.

He had learned a world of survival from the loving people in Syria and Egypt. Winnie and I did not look at each other. Brendan did not notice our reaction, but continued his tales of shimmering up to the attic when they came looking for him, of burying bruised fruits and vegetables that were unsafe to eat, of poultices and splints when bones shattered and snapped all on their own.

Brendan had lived a life of the Desert Fathers who had retreated to the desert of Egypt to be silent, simple, and solitary, wanting only to please the Lord in their penitential practices.

I invited the two Sligo men to stay the night in the men's wing of our house. Paul wanted to retire to his lorry, which he frequently slept in when his wife was 'on a tear'. Brendan slid into Garrett Kelly's bed, again spreading his long arms, perhaps embracing Garrett's ghost.

Winnie was washing up the dishes. I stood next to her and she leaned into me. "There are no mistakes in the Providence of God," she spoke softly, looking out at the black Irish night. Our spiritual director, when we were in the Novitiate during our training to be a nun, often reminded us of that. It has never wandered far from either of our thoughts.

I thought back to that day when Winnie pulled Grannie's suitcase from under her bed and showed me the money. Then the denim for our new habits. Right beyond her door stood Gino Turelli, Garrett Kelly, Jerry Muldoon, Tommy Whalen, Anne Marie Muldoon, Anne Smyth, Mary Agnes Mulvihill, Jack Kelly, and now Paul and Brendan. It is all in the Providence of God, so it is!

Chapter Twenty-Four

White Brilliance

Professor Mary Agnes Mulvihill, head of education at the new Irish university in Castletroy, Limerick, called to give her report to us. The myriad tests Deirdre took a few weeks ago were ready and she had some ideas how we could get her up to speed.

Deirdre and I were going to meet Anne Marie Muldoon and Professor Mulvihill at the Castletroy Hotel for an early dinner. Our favorite barrister had gotten the ball rolling, so we felt it only right that she should be included.

It was a few miles to the hotel, and not far from Limerick city, so our 5:00 dinner would suit us just fine. Neither of us said much in the car. Whatever the results of the test, we both understood that life in Corofin was going to change.

As we passed through Ennis, I asked Deirdre if she minded Brendan being around the house. I would hear her gasp when she would pass thought the kitchen and he was having his tea. "I guess, Fiona, it's the round ball of white hair on his old head. And him wearing Garrett's clothes."

"Have you ever just sat and joined him in his tea?" I asked her.

"Haven't time for that stuff. I got me time for Lily and my reading so I'm not forever stupid. He just sits around. Did he know Garrett? It spooks me with him just sitting around in a dead man's clothes."

"I've wondered the same. He does not talk much, so we will have to get it out of him. He has had a very strange life, as all of us have, if we're honest with each other."

"Are you calling me a liar, Fiona?"

"Calm down, Love. But to tell the truth, I think he has been around us long enough to open. It's like living with a statue, Brendan and whatever he is about."

"Fiona, do you remember that night when you and Winnie thought I had run away? I really didn't run away, and I was going to come back here to Corofin."

"So what were you doing in that God-forsaken place with those strange men by the sea?"

Deirdre said nothing and I knew not to push her, but stuff was rumbling inside her, begging to come out. I saw her look out the window at the fat sheep on the hillside, then turn her head away and cover her eyes.

"What just happened, Deirdre?" I asked her.

"I can't stand those balls of white shite, like that dirty soccer ball that came over the wall and Brendan's head, all white and round. Then those fookin' sheep are just fat balls of white shite – they make me sick.

The windshield wipers slapped away the rain, the sound hypnotizing us into calm. "Fookin' sheep" she muttered under her breath.

"So, you do not like balls of white, Deirdre?"

She did not answer, and I did not push. We would be in Castletroy in a few minutes, so I thought it better to 'let the sleeping dogs lie'.

Anne Marie and Mary Agnes Mulvihill were waiting for us in the lounge, right off the entrance. I could smell the chlorine in the pool and would have given anything to dive right in. I was getting agitated at the role-reversal, as I had sat with parents and spouses, a million times, holding all the power. Now I was powerless.

After all the pre-dinner falderal, we began eating, with the conversation tight between the two-professional woman, making Deirdre and me feel like Gypsy Rovers.

As the dishes were cleared, Professor Mulvihill spoke of Deirdre's extremely high level of intelligence, a quick mind and a rather sophisticated understand of human behavior. Common facts were missing from her repertoire, but they were easily within her reach.

She was aware that Sr. Winifred was now teaching Deirdre how to read and do math, which was wonderful. She could be ready to start college in the fall. Barrister Anne Marie interrupted, saying that Deirdre was so welcome to stay at her house during the weeks or when she travelled, because she did not like to leave the house unattended.

I graciously thanked her and told them it would all be up to Deirdre. The Professor interrupted me, inviting Anne Marie to tell us where she had been travelling.

The barrister told us that she had studied for the bar not only in Dublin, but in Oxford and Harvard. Last year she had been to Singapore, Myanmar, Pakistan, Bhopal, Sidney, Melbourne, as well as New York and London.

Deirdre pushed back from the table and looked at the ceiling. I kicked her under the table, hoping she would understand. Being impressed by someone's lies left you more than inadequate. I knew Anne Marie was deceitful.

Appropriately, we marveled at the magnificent hotel and made our way to the car. It was dark and rainy, and I was getting sleepy.

"What was that, Fiona? They are very fond of themselves and of each other."

"Why did you go up to those old mobile homes and trailers on that dirty mountainside, Deirdre? That day that you and Lily ran away from home. Tell me now, on our way back to Corofin."

Deidre began by telling me that her father, Joe Dash and his two brothers, who had appeared to get her to come home that night that Garrett chased them away, lived in that dirty place. They were into bad stuff, but she did not know what kind of bad stuff.

Now that Deirdre had a little girl herself, she wondered what had happened to her mother. There was not 'a pick of flesh' left on her bones. She was dying of cancer and Joe kicked her in the chest and stomach with his steel-toed boots and her blood was flowing onto the floor. Her mother had fallen, and he told her to stop messing it up.

Deidre never knew what had happened to her mother's poor body. She would visit her in the cemetery if she could find out where her mother was buried. With every ounce of strength in her body, she hated her father and would kill him on the spot. He was taking up too much space on the earth.

Chapter Twenty-Five

Snowballs

Brendan and I sat quietly, sipping our tea and reading the paper. I can hardly believe that Sean discovered him, rolled up in that dirty rug. Despite his occasional jerky movements, there was a deep, quiet harmony about him, like the plants that grow in the Burren.

Biddy Kelly, Jack's wife, and her sister, Kitty, came at the crack of dawn with bolts of blue denim, sewing machines, a radio, and their packed lunches. They would not hear of taking any money from us, since Jack had that cloth in the attic for years and they just wanted to be together.

Brendan went from the raggedy monk, wrapped in the rug, to this gentleman scholar who spoke little, drank gallons of tea, and was meticulous in his appearance. Brendan was easy on the nerves.

Jack Kelly pulled up to the front door and his passenger, Jerry Muldoon, knocked. Noise filled every corner of Gilhooly's home. Two more young, pregnant women, Murphy and Maude, and a woman, 'an old woman of the roads' had joined us, and the new bedrooms were filling up fast.

Jerry and Jack bustled in the front door, acting younger that they actually were. They stopped short as soon as they saw Brendan at the table. They looked at each other with their mouths wide open. Then they gave me a quick, angry look, knocking the wind out of me.

Brendan stood and introduced himself as "Brendan Foley, here for just a short time". Jerry shouted, "Where'd you get that shirt, Brendan?

"Why, in that box back where I'm staying," says Brendan, pointing vaguely to a corner in the big room.

"That does not belong to you, Brendan!" adds Jack Kelly. "That was my cousin's shirt and he wore it all the time."

Brendan's throat was reddening as he began unbuttoning the shirt.

Jack Kelly stood, a referee at the 10th round of a heavy-weight boxing match "Brendan, I am sorry. My cousin Garrett was here when the sisters came over from the States. He is not here any longer and you just gave us a fright."

"Where the hell is he? He can have his old shirt back!".

"He is not with us anymore, Brendan. I bought that shirt for him when I went to New York for conference."

"What kind of a conference?" asked Brendan.

Jack and Jerry looked at each other and then they both looked at me for help. "I'm sorry, Gentlemen, I should introduce you. This is Brendan Foley, as you know. Jack Kelly, Garrett's cousin and Jerry Muldoon, a friend of ours. Now all of you sit and have a nice cup of tea and begin all over with yourselves."

Brendan asked about the cousin and where he had gone, so they had a great, old time picking up the threads of relationships and history. Jack said that he had used a barrister, a pretty Muldoon, not like his present Muldoon company, when one of his sons got in trouble. Jerry nodded, "I know her well…we're twins.

I was fascinated, watching this boxing match. They told everything about themselves and Garrett, but not acknowledging the church connection. Just a bunch of bachelors hanging around with the nuns. Suits us just fine.

"Who is making all this racket?" Winnie shouted, making her way to the tea with her eyes half closed.

Jerry and Jack stood and kissed her soft, freckly cheek. They knew she loved them. I guess Winnie is more forthcoming, and I always hold part of myself back.

It is my hyper-vigilance, waiting for the gun to come out of my father's pocket. It is immaterial that he has been gone for 35 years. Those mountains and valleys have never left my brain.

Jack Kelly was getting restless to start measuring, drawing, counting supplies that would be needed. I gave Winnie an imperceptible nod toward the barn and she asked him when he was thinking of starting.

Jerry and Jack started toward the barn. I gave Brendan a nudge to follow. "Jack, before you get into your chapel, we first need to talk about the kitchen. We need to bump out that wall and enlarge it some. We're already too many for this compact, little room."

"She is entirely right," chirped Brendan, "some people take something I have saved for myself or they eat too much, or the little kids leave a mess and I get baby-food on my shirts."

"Whose shirts?" shouted Jerry and Jack. Brendan again started to unbutton his shirt.

"Don't be so sensitive, Old Man." Jack said almost tenderly, giving him a playful bop on his arm. "Well, the grand thing is that we have plenty of room. The Gilhooly property extends nearly 50 feet, north and west. How is the boys' section doing?"

Winnie laughed at Jack, "It's only the two of them now, a young man and an old man, so they fight it out among themselves. I never get over to that side."

Lily and Deirdre came around the side of the cabin. Lily had been walking for nearly three months. They went back to their room. Suddenly a great crash, glass shattering, Lily crying, water splashing, Deirdre screaming in Irish and English.

Jerry and I tore back to their room. Huge snowballs of white hydrangeas lay slaughtered on the floor, their necks snapped, glass from the shattered crystal vase pointing upward. Lily was sucking her thumb to console herself and Deirdre was pounding on the wall.

On the floor, amidst the broken flowers and sharp glass was a small, white greeting card:

To Deirdre

Congratulations on a job well done,

Your friend, Anne Marie Muldoon.

Chapter Twenty-Six

The Silvery Moon

The house was as still as flagstones in the Burren. Brendan was out for his evening stroll with Blacky. The mothers-to-be were relaxing in their rooms, Sean was at his homework and Deirdre and Lily were playing mini-soccer with a little pink ball in the front.

"Winnie, sit down with me. We have so little time to talk, just the two of us. Are you glad we came here, or did we make a mistake?

"I think the question we asked ourselves a year ago is: do we want to rust out or burn out? We were clear then. Has something changed your mind?"

"I guess I would like to know where we are going. I get nervous when stuff is up in the air."

"Fiona, every day of our lives is a stretch of faith. I feel we just got lifted by the Holy Spirit and dropped right, smack here, to do whatever comes our way. The Good

169

Lord is not finished with us yet, Fiona. Are you finished with Him? Or Her?"

Deirdre knocked on the door that separated us from the kitchen. "I've just put Lily down. Can I join you? I don't mean to be rude."

Winnie said she had her prayers to say and withdrew into her room. I asked why she and Lily had come in so soon. It was still light out. "That damn, big, fat, round white ball in the sky!"

"Deirdre, I think that the deep mind beneath your top mind is trying to tell you something. That is where we hide our dreams, secrets, mysteries, fears, all our history and things about our families that never got fixed. Do you want to try to listen to what your deeper mind wants to share with you? It thinks you are now ready to hear what it has to say."

"Let me think for a minute. I gotta' get some water."

***

170

"OK, let's go," she whispered under her breath. She handed me a bottle of Ballygowan still water, got herself comfortable on the soft blue couch, grabbed a yellow pillow and closed her eyes.

I asked her which trailer was hers, what color, what number, how she would get in and out, where she slept, how was it put up on the hill so it didn't roll down to the ocean, where they ate, if they had a TV.

In the back was a bunk bed. Her mother slept on the bottom and she slept on top. Her father was never home at night. Ronan, her twin brother, slept out on the couch since he was nine.

I invited Deirdre to think of the two dimensions that we would be working with: her *adult* self today and her *little girl* within. We had done a bit of work with my matryoshka, the little Russian dolls nested within each other, revealing the years and stages of life we had experienced. Now she could find out what she was hiding from herself.

I asked her to be comfortable and know she was safe with me. She was going to do some hard work that she was now ready to do. I directed her to stay in her *adult* and not slip down to her *little girl* within her. She said she would try, but would I help her if she forgot. "Of course, Deirdre, I'll remind you." I knew that dear Winnie was praying to the angels above

Gently reminding her to stay in her *adult,* sitting in our parlor in Corofin, we went to Liscannor and found her brown and yellow trailer, #5. It was cemented into the ground, so when the storms blew in from the sea, they would not go out with it. But the wind would whistle in the little windows like the Banshees screaming.

It was around Christmas, and Deirdre and Ronan had made little ornaments in school that they colored with red and green crayons. They taped them to the windows and when her father came home, he ripped them off and punched out a window over Ronan's head.

I was alert that Deirdre did not slide down to a *child* but stayed in her *adult* dimension. If she started talking baby-talk or sounded like a little girl, I would remind her right then. I knew our angels are helping Deirdre do this work. It was holy work.

I asked Deirdre to stay by the front door and just look at the spot where little Deirdre was, where was her mother, her brother and what happened when her father came in. "Stay in your *adult,* Deirdre, staying in your *adult.* Her eyes were closed, and she was observing the entire scene, showing little emotion.

I then asked her if she would be willing to take little Deirdre out of #5 and she nodded. She could pick her up or just take her by the hand and bring her to a safe place, far away from here.

Deirdre lifted her right index finger, halting my words. She had more work to do right at that spot. She was still holding the child but stood slightly back so she could watch. I would say she was almost clinical, following the action, not missing a thing.

I directed Deirdre to ask the little girl if she would like to stay there in the trailer or would like to come home with her. Deirdre nodded and held tightly to the round, yellow pillow, something material so she could physically feel that she was going out of there.

Deirdre nodded and sat, gently rocking her *little girl,* embraced by a job well done. I asked if she would like to go to bed, or if she would like to talk about what just happened. She wanted to talk.

Deirdre told me about her mother coming out of the back room, Joe Dash throwing her on the floor and kicking her to death. Ronan was not there, or he would have tried to stop him. Her mother was bleeding, trying to hold her head, making no noise. Her father shouted for her to go to bed, "get the fook out as I'm busy!"

She could see her mother go to sleep on the floor and she was bleeding terribly. Her father took a little bottle out of his pocket and had a swig. Then he laughed and pointed his finger at Deirdre, meaning the same would happen to her if she did not mind him.

Soon the uncles and his friends came in from their motorcycles to see what happened. There was a lady in a white motorcycle helmet, a big helmet, round and shiny white. She gasped!

"Fiona, I need to stop now. I am going back with Lily now. I am very tired. I just need to sleep now."

Deirdre smiled, patted me on my head, and made her way back to her sweet, quiet, peaceful room with little Lily. She was finally out of #5.

Chapter Twenty-Seven

Merry Christmas

It is another gentle morning in the Burren. I wonder how many little seeds from who-knows-where are getting ready to show off to whomever may wander, wherever they may wander.

I often think of what comes first: the personal need to wander or the rule of changing nuns and priests every number of years. It was explained that those changes were made so we did not get attached to one place. I think perhaps it was so ordained as an antidote against boredom.

Winnie has taught 2nd grade all her life. That would have driven me crazy. From age 20 to 70, she was chasing Dick and Jane, Spot and Puff, down all the years. That is fifty years, one for every bead of the rosary.

If we could line up her classes from the beginning to the end, they would begin with Irish; then Irish and Polish; then Irish, Polish, and Italian; then Polish and Mexican; then Mexican and black; then black. I guess that is why we wore black and white, a metaphor for changing neighborhoods.

If I had to pursue a study of changing neighborhoods in Chicago and Milwaukee, and probably places like Buffalo, Cleveland, Detroit, I would simply study class pictures over time at any one place.

Winnie's nature is the opposite of mine: she likes to be peaceful, prayerful, merciful; I like to be moving fast, charging at the heavy norms that have no rational, questioning. Those qualities of mine had to be held in check when I was a therapist at St. David's, an Episcopalian church in the Loop.

Deirdre comes jogging down an old country road with Lily in our old wheelbarrow. They both have a high color on their cheeks and their silken hair looks like a swirl of rich whipped cream.

"Fiona, guess what?? We just saw an old black lorry bouncing down the road with a round, white plastic ad for their services in the back. I feel so good – it was just a big, fat, round white plastic ad, that is all! Nothing to get upset about!"

"Deirdre, you did great work last night! Now your detective work is just beginning. Why don't you put Lily down for her nap and we'll finish up what you were telling me?"

She patted the top of my head again, like she did last night. I never wanted to be a dog and get lead around by a leash. I'd love to be a wild mare in the Rocky Mountains. Blacky gave me a challenging look, like I was treading on his territory with Deirdre.

She bent over to pick up Lily, "aon, do', tri', ceatha'ir, cuig" and Lily joined her in 'cuig', number 5. My heart was ready to explode with the simple 'joys of life', as the Irish say. Deirdre nudged my elbow and I knew she would be right back.

We sat outside in the lovely sun. Deirdre brought us both a bottle of Ballygowan. We could see Brendan negotiating the highways and the byways in the distance with Garrett's jeans and a white tee-shirt with Blacky by his side.

***

Deirdre started where she had finished last night. She repeated the threatening motions her father made after he had stamped out the last of her mother's life.

Then her Dash uncles came in with someone in a shiny white motorcycle helmet. They put her mother's body in a big clear plastic bag with a zipper. Deidre could look right through it until her mother's blood smeared the way.

She wished her twin brother, Ronan, had been with her. She could not figure out what was going on. They put her mother in the back of a truck that was filled with refuse and headed down to the sea. It was Christmas eve, and no one was down there, as they were all celebrating in Lahinch and Ennistymon.

Deirdre could see a small white motorboat revved up and her uncles threw her mother in the back. In the far distance, she could see big ships with all their lights on. The motorboat went out a few miles beyond the pier, turned and came back to the beach in Liscannor without her mother's body.

Her father came back to their trailer, #5 on the hill with the rest, threw some water on the floor where their mother died, grabbed a fistful of bread and waved to Deirdre, saying, "That's your Christmas present, Pet! Don't tell anyone!"

Merry Christmas, Da!

Chapter Twenty-Eight

Cheer, Cheer for Old Notre Dame

Brendan pulled into the drive in our little red Fiat. He always returned it full, no matter how long he had been out. I was still on the stoop, recovering from Deirdre's Christmas in Liscannor. He had a white envelope and asked to meet with Winnie and me.

I put on the kettle for our 99th pot of tea today and shook Winnie to get out of bed. She was completely exhausted and dreaded that new construction would soon begin, but she was excited about the larger kitchen and the new chapel.

I brought out the current cake we had the night before and set the cups and plates on the table. Brendan had on old jeans of Garrett's and a new black tee-shirt.

Emerging from the depth of sleep and a rushed dressing, Winnie's blue scapular rode high up on her neck, strangling the wind out of her. Brendan straightened it and she motioned for her tea, quickly.

I wonder if he is going to be leaving us. Where would he go? How would he live? First Garrett, now Brendan. Do we drive these guys away?

He placed the envelope on the table, moving his hand back and forth, as to whom would receive it. I nodded toward Winnie and she gulped down her tea, reached for some more and carefully opened it. She grabbed her chest, "Oh, NO!"

She slid it over to me. A check made out to the both of us for € 45,000. Allied Irish Bank. Signed Brendan Foley.

"This is at least $50,000, Brendan! Are you 'Holy Foley' who taught me at Notre Dame? Desert Fathers? Irish Monasticism? 'Holy Foley', Brendan?"

"Yes. Sister. That is what they called me. Do you think I've earned it?"

Winnie and I look at each other and then at Brendan. "What is this for, Brendan? Where did all this money come from?" asked Winnie.

"The books I've written are used all over the world in Catholic and different colleges. The order left me, I didn't leave them," stated Brendan, like a barrister.

"What about your family, Brendan? Do you have any family? Do they even have a clue about who you are and your scholarship? You've been teaching all over the world, Brendan!"

"Fiona, I have no family, except Paul who brought me down here. Paul is my son, before I even went in the order. He is well taken care of and I love him dearly, deeply, as only a father can love his own flesh and blood."

I looked for a long time at Brendan's gift. "Why are you giving this to us, Brendan? We are not charging you anything for your company. I do not want to use that old saw, 'Oh, we can never take this money,' but we can, and we will, if Winnie approves."

"Winnie and Fiona, you are doing the work of the Lord right here in the Burren. Nobody asked you to come. You were just blown by the Spirit and you had no soft landing on these hard, flat rocks!"

***

Brendan was grateful that he now was able to enter into the *Hesychasm,* the vigorous, mystical tradition of the Desert Fathers that was basic to prayer. He never had the time, place, or inclination for this arduous work. He was either teaching, writing, or simply trying to survive in the abandoned monastery up in Sligo.

As a young priest and scholar, Brendan had traveled to the ancient monasteries in the deserts of Egypt and Syria, founded by the early Christian Fathers who took the words of Jesus seriously. Anthony the Great sought perfection by selling all of his possessions, giving to the poor and following Jesus in a life of solitude, austerity, and sacrifice.

I remember well when Brendan, Holy Foley, was teaching us about the flow of Scriptural knowledge from Pachomius and Anthony, Athanasius and Macarius, to the

Celts who had been introduced in the 5th Century by Patrick to a belief in Christian spirituality.

This austerity and solitude appealed to the Druids, the Celtic priests, known for magic and wizardry. Small gatherings of monks were the beginning of the great years of Irish monasticism. The bones of these great monasteries are still left on the mountains and valleys of Ireland.

Brendan spoke often of the magnificent Book of Kells with the beautiful illustrations of birds and animals that were never seen in Ireland. Peacocks with the great sweep of their turquoise tails, jaguars, and ebony panthers, poised to attack, mother elephants, with their playful offspring.

Brendan covered his eyes. "What is Deirdre's surname? Is it Flaherty? I had a lad at Notre Dame, a Ronan Flaherty, who was from the *Gaeltacht,* the lands of Irish speakers. I think he was from the Aran Islands. I was like a father to him. We would speak Irish to each other when we were alone. Does Deirdre speak the Irish?

Chapter Twenty-Nine

Chasing after Moonbeams

A subtle bond was forming between Deirdre and Brendan. They enjoyed each other's company and could anticipate where they were going. Brendan never had a daughter; Deirdre had an evil father. Goodness played across Brendan's seasoned face like mist off the Burren.

Deirdre had begun college in Castletroy and a nest of hornets couldn't keep her home. Winnie was the main "Auntie" to Lily and I directed traffic. Jack Kelly had begun moving in tools and supplies into the barn to bump out the kitchen.

Anne Smyth from the hospital in Galway would come every Wednesday morning to check on our pregnant guests and the "Old Woman of the Road", dear Bridie Farrell, who played Mexican Train on our kitchen table every afternoon with Winnie.

We saw little of Sean Turelli who was still in school. He would petal away on the old bicycle morning, noon, and night, do his homework in his room, and get his own meals and do his own clothes. Gino Turelli had trained that lad well – he was no problem.

Brendan drove Deirdre to the college in Castletroy each morning and picked her up in the early evening. She had his ear bent with all the details of the buildings, teachers, and of her beautiful mind opening to learning.

Brendan and I were strolling around the edges of our place, as the Gardas who stopped almost daily had told us to do. Just in case there was any damage or traces of anyone trying to break in. I was glad not to go around alone.

Brendan broached the topic of Deirdre's transportation. She is maturing so fast and her mind is like a rocket. If I bring up something she has never heard, she pricks me like an old butterfly with pins stuck to her wings.

"What about going into Galway tomorrow morning, Saturday? My cousin Aiden owns Foley Fords and I know

187

he will give us a good deal on an older car, just for Deirdre. You up for it, Fiona?"

"Brendan, we can't really afford it. Your money is going to the bigger kitchen and chapel if there is any left. I would love to get her some wheels, but money is tight."

Holy Foley has it well covered. "I think the Desert Fathers would love Deirdre to have wheels! Do they really call it 'wheels' in the States?"

Winnie and Bridie were thrilled to have Lily all to themselves. Deirdre was jumping out of her skin. I sat in the back seat and let Brendan and Deirdre talk about this project.

Deirdre was excited to tells us about the garda who came to their sociology class this week. He was Sargent Foley, well over 6 feet with a flamin' red beard and a uniform fit for the Queen. His boots were like black mirrors and he stood straight as a ramrod.

Sargent Foley had been sent to head the Garda National Drug and Organized Crime Bureau of the North Western part of Ireland. We had become the entrance for the "whole, entire, complete - north, south, east and west - of every single part of Europe! For our drugs!

Because our rivers and beaches and empty little villages right on the rugged coasts of Mayo, Galway, Kerry, Cork, including Clare, were ideal for ships to connect with smaller vessels to sneak the drugs right into Ireland. The Irish gangs controlled the little trawlers, even rowboats, big and small yachts, power boats. curraches, the Galway Hookers with their deep brownish-red sails that bring tears to your eyes.

Deirdre could not imagine the breadth and width of this massive, global problem that landed right here in our backyard. Her little hands kept expanding and contracting as she demonstrated all that she had heard.

"They come from Venezula, Brazil, Mexico, and even Pakistan, Morocco, Korea, India, all just to us, because we have always known how to handle the seas, the rough and dangerous waters, the sharp, stony cliffs, storms and gale winds. There is nothing we can't do, because I'm from Kilrowan, right out there on those islands! I know water, alright!

"First it was probably just weed, then soon dope and heroin, cocaine, uppers like speed and bennies, meth, Ecstasy, angel dust, mushrooms! Wow!! Just to little old Ireland, the 'land of saints and scholars'!"

Brendan looked at her through his sunglasses that had slid down his long nose. "Deirdre, you sound like you are proud of us, being the eye of the storm for all of Europe:

"Oh, Jaycus, God Almighty, Brendan, it is terrible what we've gotten ourselves into! Just terrible, terrible, terrible!!"

After all the 'to-ing and fro-ing' about the car, Brendan drove it home and I drove our car. Deirdre was still into our new place in the world. "Fiona, you know how you get mad when women are not treated right, or people think we're stupid? Well, you'll never guess who is in charge of all this drug stuff??"

I shook my head, as if I would know anything about it. "AN IRISH WOMAN THEY CALL THE DRAGON LADY!!"

Chapter Thirty

The Old Woman of the Roads

The back wall in our kitchen had disappeared, leaving Winnie and Bridie playing their Mexican Train beside the night sky. Lily would not be excluded, so she was teething on little slices of apple and drooling all over her highchair.

Bridie and Winnie also had a language between them, which I feel is about the compatibility of their personal energy or of the currents of their souls. They simply *got* each other in a language that defies words. That must be 'love at first sight'.

I would watch them go off over the Burren, arms linked together like the women over here do, pushing Lily between them. Lily in her wobbly wicker pram, trying to catch Blacky as he raced beside her.

Winnie had an intuitive way about her. She could storm through reluctance without clearing her throat. Her mother would do that and none of the O'Grady kids could lie to her. It was like a moan, peppered with curiosity, that melted resistance.

Bridie was isolated for many weeks in her little room at the end of the hall. We knew nothing about her and did not want to break her self-cloistering. I felt she just needed that for a while. Deirdre took it upon herself to see that Bridie was fed and clean.

In short, Bridie's story came tumbling out, little piece by little piece, but it felt like a 'hurricane' to her, as she had contained it for most of her life. Perhaps the truth does make us free.

Anne Smyth, our Galway Hospital nurse, informed us, with Bridie's consent, that most of her skin was marbled, pink and white, like a Greek statue. There had been a terrible fire. A terrible, terrible fire; Anne knew none of the details.

She had never disclosed this to anyone, but since the moans out of Winnie sounded like an oboe, Bridie took the invitation and decided to invite Winnie to the story of her tragic life. Bridie welcomed me to sit down as she began her story.

Bridie Farrell was born into a fierce IRA family up in Killybegs in the County of Donegal. On a political fashion, it was in the Republic of Ireland; geographically, it was farther north than Co. Fermanagh, Tyrone, and parts of Londonderry, (called Derry by Catholics) in Ulster.

Bridie was born long before the Troubles, but there were always troubles between the Protestants and the Catholics. She fell madly in love with William Campbell, who 'kicked with his left foot', a cloaked way of saying he was Protestant, not Catholic 'at all, at all'.

The Farrells were many, scattered up and down Killybegs Township, and not one Farrell had ever deserted the church or the IRA. If anyone were caught in disloyalty, they would say 'sure, you're shaming the Mighty Farrells!'

Wild horses could not pull Bridie and William away from each other. Her family hated Protestants; his family hated Catholics. There was no place to wiggle between them. Neither family attended the small wedding by the local judge. Bridie had seven sisters and eight brothers, all with large families, but none of them appeared.

So, Bridie at 17 and William at 18 took off with nothing but the love in their hearts and a farewell to their small-hearted, nasty families. With a small inheritance from his grandmother, William bough a small farm in Dunshambro, in Co. Leitrim. Bridie taught William how to work and William taught Bridie how to be his wife.

Soon the small thatched cabin was filled with seven children, glorious creatures who caught all the loved that splashed about from the love between Bridie and William. The seven children - four boys and three girls - felt loved, safe, and happy.

Bridie and William knew they had done the right thing and prayed only prayers of gratitude as they went about chores on their small farm. They both had inherited happy dispositions and seemingly, all of the Campbell children had it in their genes.

The summer had been dry, with only a whiff of rain early in the mornings on the banks of the lovely Lough

Allen that splashed against the Iron Mountains. A stack of turf was drying against the house, ready to warm them at evening with a quiet, glowing fire.

Every night before she went to bed, Bridie banked the glowing bricks of turf, ready for the morning. It was a tradition that the mother of every family would stack the turf in the center of the hearth, so the flame would never go out.

Brigid was the goddess of the hearth in pagan days and later, St. Brigid's cross, made of wisps from the willow tree, was hung to prevent fires. The family of Bridie and William hung a Brigid's cross over their door.

The bluebells that grew around the cabin had never been so blue and the apple and pear trees were heavy with young fruit. Maddie Campbell, the youngest, would gather a small handful of bluebells for her mother and Bridie placed them in a small jelly jar in the middle of their table.

Bridie slipped out of bed and before she headed down to Lough Allen for her evening bath in the fresh spring waters, she checked the hearth. As the lack of rain had caused the thatch roof to become dry, she could hear the bluebirds throughout the day, singing to one another and to all the Campbells below.

As she looked into the glowing embers, she was concerned as throughout the day, little snippets of turf, hay or even cloth would alight and lift in the air. She had even burned her hand on one little such particle. The fire now looked quiet, no strange wisps looking to catch fire.

Bridie grabbed herself the big light blue towel and walked by the light of the full moon down to Lough Allen to bathe like a Gypsy Rover. The children and William were sleeping soundly, the warm summer days taking all their energy in work and play.

A dark owl looked down at her as she dove into the cool waters. Her heart embraced the peace that surrounded the night. Bridie's prayer was one of profound gratitude for her many blessings, eight of whom were sound asleep up the hill. She was thankful for these few quiet minutes by herself, that happen not often.

With a smile that broke across her young face, Bridie looked up the hill. She screamed from her toes to her head. The owl flew in the other direction. The cabin was a ball of fire. Like a wild woman, she tore up the hill, naked and screaming.

Thatched cottages were always consumed in a matter of a very few minutes. She ran inside and there were no signs of life, no sounds of anyone beside herself.

In a trance, she walked on the smoldering coals to the small beds and cots and mounds of blankets that her children slept in. She crawled on the dirt floor to William's body and lay beside the hot, darkened flesh of her lover.

Bridie rose and walked down to Lough Allen for her clothes. She opened the strong gate that William had made with the boys and let the cows free. She chased the chicken and goats and sheep up onto Iron Mountain, praying that they be safe.

Mary, the fluffy, strapping English sheep dog followed Bridie down the narrow path and they walked together on the highways and byways of her beloved country for nearly 30 years, until she came to Corofin and met her soul-mate Sister Winnie O'Grady.

Chapter Thirty-One

On the 50-yard-Line

Lily and I were enjoying *"One Fish, Two Fish, Red Fish, BluFish"* and at 18 months, she was an excellent reader, or so I told her mother. Brendan was still running Deirdre into school, as she had yet to obtain her driver's license.

The phone rang and a voice announced, "Jeremiah Muldoon, bishop of Galway". I did not know if I should fall on my knees or just laugh. Poor woman, I simply invited her to put him on.

"Jerry, morning greetings! Have not seen you since our momentous decision about our tiny kitchen. How've you been keeping?"

"Fiona, it's wonderful to hear your voice and your Chicago accent. Any news from Gino Turelli?"

"I think he's rounding up some strays and they will be swinging hammers over here in no time. I really think he wants to get his Sean home with all the rest of them. He's too young to go on by himself."

Jerry asked if he and his sister, 'Her Highness, the Barrister Anne Marie Muldoon' could come out for dinner sometime this week. They had something on the backburner that was coming to the front.

"Tonight will be perfect, Jerry. Lily is the only one home, but she'll have your tea ready at the strike of six."

I put little notes about the Muldoon's coming for dinner up at the front and back doors, opened the frig and wondered what we would have for dinner. I will have to rouse Winnie and we will both go into Ennis to the grocery store. We will have to take the Boss with us, or she will be so lonesome.

***

Winnie turned to me in Dunne's parking lot. We had placed our bags in the "boot"; I still have to make a conscious effort not to say "trunk". Lily was getting cranky, as she had to sit alone in the back in her car seat and not up front with us big girls.

"So, what's up with our friends?", Winnie asked, her right arm back to hold Lily's foot.

"Damned if I know. They have been awfully quiet lately. We will soon know. Do you want to take the lead?"

"NO" rang Winnie, clear as a bell.

"I'd really like everyone to be present tonight. Minus the two girls having babies. I would really like to get to know Murphy and Maude. Pray that they have safe deliveries. I am so glad that we know Anne Smyth."

"She's a God-send, Fiona. I just found out that Bridie Farrell cured her own burns that covered her entire body with buttermilk. Every morning, she and Mary would stop at a friendly door and get a cup of it and she would spill it on herself, because her body was too sore to touch. Especially her shoulders.

"I definitely want Bridie to be with us tonight. Tell her she has nothing to fear and forget their high and mighty positions – that is not who they really are and there's no fear of them."

"How about giving me one little degree of common sense, Fiona? Of all she has been through, do you think Bridie would be intimidated by the high and mighty?

Besides, the Muldoons are a fine family and there is no fear of them at all," trumpeted Winnie.

We gathered in the kitchen a bit before 6:00, as everyone was hungry and anxious to know who was coming? Lily stood tall, as an important member of our wobbly family.

I told them that both Murph and Maude had baby boys and they were all doing fine. It does not hurt to have the head nurse looking after them. Right from the beginning, Anne Smyth approached us with an understanding of shared responsibility.

I spoke to our little family about the Muldoons and made it clear we were not to treat them as celebrities, they were simply our friends. I was not privy to their agenda.

The meal with three plump chickens and stuffing, lots and lots of buttery potatoes, bright peas and carrots, fresh butter and cream, sliced tomatoes, brown bread.

Without a word, Sean cleared the dishes, rinsed them, and put them in the dishwasher. On the stove sat a nice, fat pot of hot tea and Deirdre had the warm bread pudding from the oven in bowls for us in a flash. Bird's Custard dripped down the sides of the pudding.

As we began our desert, Jerry told us that they had some concerns in the Galway diocese. Many of the old priests had nowhere to go. Parishes could not keep up the priests' houses with their housekeepers and cooks, and their families really did not want them to come home, after all the reports on some of their behaviors.

Anne Marie placed her thin hand on his and tapped for a short while. She wanted to talk. "Now, friends, we have the resources to more than cover their expenses, and we would love to see them at home here. We need to put another extension projecting out from the male side of the house."

"Right at this moment there are seven priests that are homeless. After Casey, our funds dried up 'like a raisin in the sun'. The home for old priests was shuttered within three years and we're going to have to import priests from Poland and Africa," Jerry moaned.

Anne Marie nudged her brother with her elbow. "Jerry, why don't we take a nice walk around the Burren and let them talk. They need their privacy."

"That is the last thing we need, Anne Marie. We need to discuss this among ourselves with no secrets, no surprises, no shocks. You are most welcome to stay here, as you and your brother are an important part of who we are. What do we think?"

Winnie drew a loud sip of her tea, placed her tea mug squarely adjacent to her plate, and began "With all serious deference to you, Bishop Muldoon, the very last thing I ever want to do is to spend a single day with a priest. Excluding you and Brendan, of course."

"And Irish priests are the very worst," chirped Bridie, "they get themselves mixed up with God."

Sean put on his most innocent face, "I'm going to exclude myself from this discussion. I think I'm too young and I'm American."

"Just a minute, young man! Do you live here? OK, this has nothing to do with your uncle, Garrett Kelly. Step up to the plate, Sean!"

"Then my answer is NO".

"I'd leave," whispered Deirdre, "and take her with me," nodding to the little tike in her highchair.

Brendan did not speak yet, but I had very strong feelings that the priests had been trained, brain-washed, to think they were special and deserving of favorites. If Jesus himself came down to them, they would not understand what it means to be a *Wounded Healer*.

I asked Brendan if he would like to speak. Brendan shook his beautiful mane of white hair, extending his ten nobly fingers on the table, palms down. We understood his position.

Little Lily shrieked and laughed at her private joke, whispered in her little ear by her Guardian Angel.

Chapter Thirty-Two

The Girl from Aran

Before Deirdre could get her driver's license, we needed her birth certificate. She had none. Baptismal certificate? Entering school? Census? Nothing.

Jerry had arranged with the head of the Connaught North-West division to issue a birth certificate to the name of Deirdre Flaherty, born November 15, 1996, to parents Lily Flaherty and Joe Dash, Aran Islands, County Galway.

We were looking for a bit of privacy. It was so strange how people would look at Winnie and me in our blue-jean habits, as if they had never seen a nun. It is true, we were obsolete: the young people were born after we disappeared; the older people thought they were seeing a mirage. (And would slip us a Euro or two in appreciation for just being there.)

The Aran Islands were simply an extension of the Burren, covered with limestone from millions and millions of years ago. There was no land, just rocks that were used as boundaries.

I had been there many years before Deirdre was born. The whole place looked like lacy squares and rectangles, all blackish gray from the sharp, flat stones, the gray sand, gray rain and sea water, blackish gray people, bogged down with the sadness of the hard, flat place. It made me want to scream. I had to get off before I lost my mind. I did not share this with Deirdre.

We found a small off-beat coffee shop near Galway Bay so I could get a sense of who Deirdre really was. Her mother was Lily and all seven of her brothers had been lost at sea. Her grandmother was Mary Flaherty, a mighty woman who buried her husband and her seven sons and was left with only her daughter, Lily Flaherty.

They were fishermen, going out in their feather-weight boats, called *curraches,* that understood the sea better than any man. They were so light that Winnie and I could have hoisted it up on our heads and walk into the surf. And drowned.

Deirdre was delighted with herself that she could tell her story to me. As the Aran Islands were part of the Gaeltacht, Irish was the first language that Deirdre learned.

There were three islands and the Flahertys lived on the largest, *Inishmoor.*

They say that the sky is thin there, and the place is closer to heaven. They say you can lift your arm and touch the very Face of God. I think the Burren is much that same way, as the large, long stones are simply an extension of the Aran Isles.

She slipped between the Irish and English unconsciously, and when she was speaking in Irish, I would just listen to those rolling consonants and stranger vowels and think back to Grannie and Uncle Jack Gilhooly, going at each other in Irish, right in our kitchen.

Deirdre's grandmother, Mary Flaherty, had buried first her husband Tom, barely 30 years old, then her seven boys, and before Ronan, the last son, got in his currach, he helped the neighbors to make his own coffin.

After Ronan was buried, Mary, with her brilliant red skirt and plaid shawl tight around her head and shoulders, took herself up to the historic stone fort, Dun Aengus, early one Saturday morning and hurled herself into the sea.

Three rough men came to their island soon after. The people did not like these men, as they were ugly, loud, and dirty. They had a speedboat and they terrorized the children and made fun of the way they talked.

Lily, Deirdre's mother, was alone with only one neighbor, an old man who talked to the gulls who would swoop the bread out of his hand when he was fishing. She was frightened of him.

So those strangers sensed that Lily was alone and while the other two watch from the door of her hovel, the big one, Joe, had his way with her and raped her over and over. This on top of losing all of her brothers and parents.

When the men in the village realized that they had not protected young Lily, they came to get them. His brothers at the door yelled to Joe and they each slid down the shortest cliff, got their boat and motored to the mainland.

Nine months later, Deirdre and her brother Ronan were born. Her mother was helped by the midwife who was excited about delivering twins. Deirdre said that her mother was the best mother and taught them all she knew. She just knew the Irish, not English.

They ran around the island like wild sheep, slipping and sliding on the seaweed, rolling into the sea like billiard balls. The seaweed was slippery because the mackerel was oily and that made the ocean oily.

Their world was rainy and foggy and misty and they had sharp eyes and ears so they would know if anyone was around them that should not be.

One day when they were about six or seven, the three ugly men came for them. They pointed guns at them and made Lily and Ronan slide down the short cliff. Then they threw the little family into their dirty boat and took off for the beach in Liscannor.

They chased them up to the brown and yellow trailer, #5. Joe told Lily that she was his wife and the twins' father. She had to cook for them and be his wife and never talk to him unless he first talked to her. Deirdre and her brother hated him.

Soon a Yank, our Uncle Pat, took Ronan with him and told her that he would come back for her. He never did.

211

Ronan does not even know that their mother was murdered and where she is now. Ronan will kill him if he ever finds out.

I am concerned that Deirdre will breakdown when she sees her birth certificate. The fact that Joe Dash is listed as 'husband' and 'father' might just throw her over, like sliding and slithering on the greasy seaweed with nothing to break her fall.

"Deirdre, we need to thank Jerry. It's nice to have friends in high places, isn't it?", I asked her, finishing my coffee.

"I don't like her," she finished our conversation.

Chapter Thirty-Three

No Place Like Home

After we picked up Deirdre's birth certificate and beginner's permit to drive, we were both tired and said little. They call this 'companionable silence'.

"I'd like to invite Paul for dinner, Fiona. Would that be ok?"

"Whoa…what's going on, Deirdre?"

"Remember, I told you about him. He is a garda. He spoke to our sociology class about the drug problem up and down the West Coast of Ireland and how drugs come in here from all over the world and are sold all over Europe from right here. Kids are dying with needles in their arms. Did you know that there are ten Irish gangs who do this stuff?"

"I had no idea. And in this spot? Paul Foley?"

"Fiona, they had cocaine worth 5 million Euros stuck in a torpedo shell that came flying up to the beach right in Liscannor. You know who that made me think of?"

213

"Let us get back to Paul Foley. You'll have to check with Brendan."

"Why?"

"Paul is his son."

"I thought priests weren't supposed to have sex. Did he get permission from the Pope or something like that?"

"I didn't ask him."

"Brendan doesn't seem much like a priest that's fat and drinks. Remember that night we found him rolled up in that dirty rug. They should take better care of people like Brendan."

"Deirdre, that's what we do. The young man who drove that truck is his son, Paul Foley. Brendan had a girlfriend before he became a priest. You know the rest.

Deirdre told me that Paul came to the college to see her. He got her schedule from Professor Mary Agnes Mulvihill, that pal of Anne Marie. He wanted to know if I knew any kids who were smart, still spoke Irish, and wanted to help the Garda.

"I gave him a big smile and pointed to myself. He just shook his head and said he needed one of the lads. I told him I was the best.

I then I asked her why they were looking for Irish speakers. Apparently, some of this business is being conducted by gangs from the islands and Connemara. It is very secret. The ideal person would be an islander with education, preferably in the law, and unable to be compromised with the money.

Deirdre gasped, "My brother Ronan! He is now with the FBI in Chicago! I'll grab Conneely next time I see him. He writes letters to Ronan and that is how I keep track of him. Ronan thinks if he writes directly to me, Joe Dash will kill me, just like he did to our poor, sick Mammie."

"Deirdre, this sounds too urgent to wait until you bump into Conneely. Where does he live? Is he a good guy?"

"In Kilrush, near where Paul Foley sleeps, right above Jack Kelly's hardware store. I see his truck out here now and then and it just reminds me of Garrett before he got killed."

"Why don't we toddle into Kilrush right now – it's not far, and we'll be making Paul Foley's job easier for him."

"Ohhhh, this is so exciting!!"

"Hold your horses, Deirdre! What does this Conneely look like? Tall or short? Fat or Skinny? Smart or dumb?"

***

I called Winnie and told her that Deidre and I "were on a mission from God", just like the Blues Brothers and we might be late coming home for dinner. She was fine with that. Bridie was finally *warming* up to Lily.

We just turned into the big square in Kilrush when Deirdre spotted Seamus Conneely crawling out of a pub. She whistled and he came right to the car. Seamus reached into his pocket and pulled out a ball of paper, Ronan's last letter to Seamus.

Deirdre grabbed it out of his hand and told him she would return it at school. He shared with us that after Ronan graduated from Notre Dame, his uncle Pat wanted him to stay right there and get his law degree. It is different over in the States, she informed me. I nodded. I dare not disagree at this fork in the road.

Seamus told us that Ronan had just finished law school, passed the bar and Uncle Pat grabbed him for the FBI. He had to go to their academy in Quantico, Virginia for special training to be an agent. They wrote to each other in Irish so Ronan would not forget it.

The following week, Sargent Paul Foley joined us for dinner. I nearly forgot how big a man he is – taller than his father and filled out in muscle and nerve.

Both Brendan and Deirdre met him at the door. He kissed his father first and Deirdre rolled her eyes. Lily barged right up to Paul and fell back when she saw his size. She started to cry from the fright of him. He was still in his blue uniform, so that made him all the more imposing.

After Deirdre introduced him to us, I asked him where his wife was. He scratched his head. "Remember,

Paul, you said that you always slept in your lorry when 'your wife was on a tear'." He winked down at Lily who was warming up to him. "I was trying to be polite, that's all, Deirdre. No wife."

The table was set in the kitchen, as that was the only large table we had. We had the same meal that we had for Jerry and Anne Marie only a few weeks ago. We ate our dinner quietly, as Paul Foley took up a lot of space. Brendan beamed with pride at his son, right here with us.

I told Paul that his father taught me at Notre Dame, and he nodded as he braved another chicken leg. Brendan studied his plate with the soft carrots, floating in butter and parsley flakes. Little Lily scowled at me and gave out one of her most delightful screams. The kid did not miss a trick, just like her mother.

We grew quiet again. Soon there were motorcycles gunning their motors in our drive. Deirdre squeezed Paul's thick, bulging arms and shouted, "It's the Dashes! For the love of God, Paul, stop eating and get up and do something!"

Young Sean bolted into the barn and reached for his father's gun, hidden in a black Kelly Hardware shirt. Gino had left it there for our protection. Sean ran down the hall after Paul and thrust the loaded gun in his hand. The Garda do not regularly carry guns.

With both of his massive hands, Paul aimed the pistol right at the three men who had come for Deirdre and Lily. He shouted in Irish that he will have them in prison next time he sees them. Paul absolutely forbid them to be within 100 feet of Deirdre and Lily.

He then shot three times over their heads and they whipped around and tore out of the Burren.

Brendan put his arms around Paul and Paul put his arms around Deirdre and Lily. Bridie and Winnie locked arms and returned to the kitchen. I gave Sean a soft hug, as he was wise beyond his years.

Chapter Thirty-Four

Gathering the Loose Ends

Deirdre was meeting Anne Marie Muldoon for lunch in Castletroy. She passed her driving test, found a small job at the college, and took care of her own expenses with her car and clothing.

Through Sargent Paul Foley, she was able to call her brother Ronan at the FBI. I placed the call from our house in the kitchen. They had not talked in over twelve years. She told him that their poor, sick mother had died when they were 12, but Ronan had left the year before with their uncle, Pat Flaherty.

"Dash?" Ronan asked his sister.

"Yeah," she responded.

There was a long silence between them. Deirdre thought that Ronan must have known, but still it was a shock to say and hear the words. They whispered 'good-by' and hung up.

Deirdre sat with her face in her hands, trying to grab her breath. I poured her a cup of hot tea and gave her biscuits on a small plate. Despite her gaping lack of formal education, Deirdre was one of the brightest persons I had ever met.

So often I would picture her back on *Inishmoor,* with her head covered, walking in the rain and mist and fog, bare feet, and using all her instincts to stay safe. She had an internal radar system that never failed her. Did Ronan have it too?

When she raised her head, she had a strange, somewhat glowing expression on her face. "I'm so proud of him, finishing school and law school and going to be a barrister, just like 'you know who', but he'll be so good and help people. I just wish he were here with us."

"What's with you and Anne Marie?"

"She just smells funny to me. I think she's a phony."

We had so many irons in the fire, that if we crossed Anne Marie, we'd lose Jerry and if we lost Jerry, we'd lose poor Garrett Kelly and then Jack Kelly, his wife, Kitty, and her sister, Biddy. Then Professor Mulvihill and Nurse Anne Smyth.

Then Deirdre was totally gone with Sgt. Paul Foley, and then Brendan, Winnie and Bridie, her own Lucy, her brother Ronan and Seamus Conneely.

When I was younger, I thought the right thing was to always stay in the middle. Not to take sides. Remain neutral. Indifferent to power grabs. Do not try to explain unconscious drives and reasoning. Stay everyone's friend. Make no enemies.

I was wrong on every single aspect of my neutrality. It never worked and really, it was such an infantile thing to do. I know that Anne Marie puts Deirdre's teeth on edge, and I respect that 3rd eye that Deirdre has.

It feels to Deirdre that Anne Marie is "courting her". She showed Deirdre her palatial house in Castletroy with paintings and crystal and china from all over the world. Deirdre questioned me about how much money she makes as a barrister, since she can afford all this stuff.

They dine at the fanciest places and she tells Deirdre to order the most expensive food on the menu.

Professor Mulvihill sometimes joins them, and sometimes Anne Smyth from the Galway hospital who took care of her and Lucy 'that night'.

Deirdre does not like the way Anne Marie looks at her, almost like she is in love with Deirdre. She never talks about any boyfriends, just "Jerry this and Jerry that".

"So why do you hang out with her?" I asked. It felt so contradictory, yet I trusted Deirdre's radar system. She had an uncompromising morality and would simply not be using Anne Marie for money; so, going against her nature must have been a higher calling than just cutting her lose because she 'smelled funny'.

That night I prayed to St. Michael the Archangel to protect young Deirdre, who had fire in her belly. I am glad that I am not Anne Marie Muldoon, Barrister, sister of Jerry Muldoon, Bishop of Galway. I am glad that I am just me.

Chapter Thirty-Five

Sherlock Holmes

Sargent Paul Foley gave Deirdre a phone used by the Gardas. If an under-cover agent were feeling uncertain about a stake-out, he would send an active conversation back to the Garda station, so he was covered.

Deirdre was asked to stay the night with Anne Marie. I knew she was nervous, but I knew she was restless like I used to get when I was younger. Now all I want is peace and quiet, not actions and reactions.

We had a system that when she wanted me to be with her and listen to what she and Anne Marie were saying, she would push the small blue button on the phone, and it would come into my phone.

On Fridays, Deirdre would finish school at 3:00. She had her own car, her driver's license, and a full tank of petrol, as they say over here. She had packed a small overnight bag, so she was all set. I was uneasy for her.

Anne Marie had given her a key to the side door, so Deirdre let herself in, brought her things to the guest room and made a pot of tea, waiting for Anne Marie. It was dark with the heavy trees that sheltered her house.

Deirdre called me. "Fiona, I'm still alone here. I would never want to live with all this crap. There are Persian rugs on top of Persian rugs, pictures of sail boats, yachts, big ocean steamers. She has a big, whale harpoon on her dining room wall. Starfish and conch shells on the tables.

"I'm now looking at her built-in bookcases and there is nothing about the law and what a barrister would be interested in. Just about sailing."

"Deirdre, use your phone and take pictures of her books. Then send them right back over to me. Don't delete any of them."

Within a few minutes, pictures of books entitled: *Climatology Handbook; Wind Sailing Vectors; Study of Wave Forecasting Methodology; The Barometer at Sea; Maritime Meteorology; Understanding Ocean Weather; Nautical Monographs* flew over the Burren to me.

The thick fog, mist and ghosts out on the Aran Islands far from here, sharpened Deirdre's instincts to negotiate through the haze, relying on her instincts and her angels and her brother Ronan to protect her from a deadly wave, a blow to her head, a tumble off her donkey onto the flat, sharp, lacy stones.

I had to trust Deirdre to do the job she assigned to herself and to know she was far cleverer than I to go where she is being led. I do not trust Anne Marie either.

I did not hear anymore from Deirdre that evening, but when she returned home later that night, she said that she walked into the kitchen later that night and Anne Marie was dressed in her horse-hair white wig and her unbuttoned black barrister robe, with nothing underneath.

Deirdre quickly excused herself and made for the guest room. Anne Marie followed her, wanting to know what was wrong. Deirdre snapped off the light and told her that she felt a migraine headache on the way, and she had to get to bed.

Deirdre heard Anne Marie go to bed, but she was too distraught to sleep. Soon Anne Marie was snoring.

Deirdre threw books and everything, especially her phone, in her bag, slid open the window and dropped down to the grass.

She almost twisted her ankle, falling on top of a white motorcycle, parked under the bedroom window. Deirdre propped herself against the cycle to get up, touching a big, round, shiny white helmet, hanging from the handlebars. She gasped. It all fell into place, like a thousand-piece jig-saw puzzle.

Deirdre ran to her little yellow Bug, threw her bag in the front seat next to her and sped out of the drive. As she shifted gears, she looked back to the house. Anne Marie was waving good night.

She flew back to the Ennis Road and was back home within less than ½ hour. Deirdre ran to the front door and it was locked. She looked back to the road and there was no trace of any other cars. She knocked softly and Winnie was there in no time. She was getting a glass of milk in the kitchen.

Deirdre fell into Winnie's arms, shaking and stuttering, slipping into Irish, then back to English, then

227

Irish again. Bridie was sleeping with Lily, so Winnie brought Deirdre back into the kitchen for current cake and a glass of rich, creamy milk.

I joined them, as Winnie said that she knew Deirdre had been seeing things and it upset her terribly. Winnie understood that it was both a blessing and a curse; it was difficult to talk about it without people laughing.

Deirdre wiped a tear and began, "I keep seeing Liscannor beach, pitch dark, but lights shine brightly on a yacht bumping into the pier and RIGs are floating everywhere and I hear gun-shots and Anne Marie is walking on top of the water like Jesus did in the storm and she's laughing and laughing and Jerry, her brother, is drowning off beyond the pier.

Winnie put her gnarled old hand on top of Deirdre's young hand. She looked at her with the beginning of a smile, "Deirdre, Love, we are just going to put your scary vision right smack in the hands of Our Lord. You have a gift that you did not ask for and there are many, many people on your team. You go back now with Lily and get yourself some sleep."

"OK, Winnie, but before I go, I have to tell you that that is the only house in Ireland that does not have pictures of Jesus and Mary, the pope, and of John and Jackie Kennedy. Just boats."

Deirdre gasped and ran to open her blue bag. She pulled out a black ledger book that she had taken from Anne Marie's house. She opened it while Winnie and I were still at the kitchen table.

"There are ten or twelve of these under the bed in the guest room where I was to sleep. There is a fancy thing that hangs down to the floor, so you do not see under the bed, but I had a coin that rolled under and I had to get it back. Just look!! They are all written in Irish!"

While my Irish is none, Deirdre ran her fingers down the columns, reading off the names of boats in Irish, then translating. There were columns for temperature, height of waves, wind velocity, weight of ship, what it was carrying: h for heroin; c for cocaine; a for amphetamines; o for opioids; m for marijuana.

Winnie held both her hands and smiled. "Deirdre, you've struck gold!! This is why you were over there. We will meet with the Garda tomorrow and share this with them. You have made Paul Foley's job a lot easier! Is this what they taught you out on the island?"

I looked at the clock. It was nearing 3:00 a.m. "Let's try and get some sleep. We'll have a big day tomorrow", I whispered.

"Give me one more second, Fiona. She has a big, round, bright, white motorcycle helmet hanging from the bars of her cycle. That is what I have been seeing. The bitch was there years ago to drag my mammie out, sick, dead, and bloody that Christmas Eve. I know it was her."

I put my arms around her frail body, breathed in her strong spirit, and guided her off to bed.

Chapter Thirty-Six

The Grand Finale

We were up very early, even though we did not get to bed until after 3:00 a.m. When Winnie and I came here, we had no definite plans, just responding to the breathing of the Spirit, moving us on.

When we speak about Garrett Kelly, his Covenant with God always breaks into the conversation. I do not know if one moment, you have no Covenant with God; then in the next moment, it is established. Or if simply by our creation, God fulfills his or her part and the rest is up to us. That sounds better.

Sgt. Paul Foley is meeting with us this morning to hear what happened with Anne Marie yesterday and to examine her ledger. Before we came, I thought we would be sitting in two rockers, watching the turf smoke curl above the thatched cottages, waiting for God's Holy Angels to carry us to the Rapture.

We are about to cross a threshold, and nothing will ever be the same. Winnie and I have not been passive observers, but critical players, sometimes just clearing a way for the younger ones.

Lily met Paul with one piercing shriek, as he lifted her upon his shoulders to touch the ceiling. Deirdre put her head onto his chest and Brendan patted his son's back.

Paul could not get his hands on the ledger fast enough. I watched his large hands tremor as he stabilized the heavy book on his knees and began turning pages.

Terms like money laundering, Irish gangs, psychotropic drugs, RIBs, Glock 24, Pele box, Azores High, and North Atlantic Drift are foreign to us. This is very serious business and involves millions and millions of dollars or Pounds or Euros.

This 'little piece of heaven that fell from out the sky one day' is located in the most strategic place on the planet and within the easiest point for distribution. The entire West Coast is fringed with rugged, raggedy in-lets and out-lets. The Garda and National Drug enforcement agencies are short-handed and unsophisticated against the drug runners.

It is nearly impossible to police the rough and often violent waters. The West Coast gets hit right in the face with winds and waves, storms and savage weather that provide a familiar protection to the drug gangs.

If bales of cocaine get washed overboard, the industrious felons get in their little rigid inflatable boats (RIB) and secure their precious cargo. I get the sense that since Ireland is so open, the bad guys are laughing right in the face of the Garda.

And the Garda are essentially helpless to stop this drug tsunami for claiming our sacred territory for itself. It is a 'walk in the park', as nine out of ten drug runners are successful, and they can unload their tons of wares in Ireland to be sold throughout the world.

Who among us would report on the vicious gangs, perhaps involving our own sons and brothers and husbands? As the impotence of the Garda is so evident, who would trust them with critical information? Maybe Paul Foley is different.

***

In a strange way, we were quiet. Bridie looked at Winnie and Winnie shrugged her shoulders. Brendan's hands were steepled in front of his face. Was he praying? Sean was growing restless, in that twilight zone between youth and adult. Lily needed her nappy changed.

"Pardon me, folks, but I've got to run. I do not mean to be rude. Duty calls!", explained Paul as he untangled his legs, grabbed his keys, kissed Brendan on his rough cheek, squeezed Deirdre's shoulder, waved at the rest of us and was off.

With a look of smug satisfaction, Deirdre held our attention. "Paul forgot that I read Irish. A big shipment of heroin is arriving from Pakistan after 8:00 tonight. I am sure Anne Marie Muldoon, the Barrister, will be sailing her *Maid of the Midst* out to meet that stuff. I bet Joe Dash and the guys will be with her, ready with their RIBS"

"*Maid of the Midst* is that pleasure boat they use at Niagara Falls," I offered. "So how about we make some plans? Any ideas?"

Winnie semi-raised her hand, like she was back in 2nd grade. "Do we call Jerry Muldoon? She's his sister, after all."

"How many lives, how many families has she destroyed? If Jerry knows what's happening, he will have to alert her, and everything would be off, and the Dragon Queen would live to welcome another ship of shit for our kids." Deirdre closed her eyes and shook her head.

"Do you think we could just show up without ruining it for the Garda? What about Lily? How many cars? Should we just skip it?" Deirdre asked.

"Fiona, Bridie and Lily and I are staying home for Lawrence Welk and we'll make popcorn. Everyone is welcome to join us. And if you guys go too early, Paul Foley will send you home," Winnie assured us.

Deirdre cleared her throat. "OK, here's the plan. We eat plenty about half-six. We leave here in one car and we can park in the lot for the Cliffs of Moher. I know the guy who runs it. We can take turns watching out for the Dragon Queen and her yacht.

"Then we'll go in the dark the way down the back of the Cliffs. Dress warmly - something on your heads and ears, warm socks and boots, gloves. Brendan, you driving?"

The day passed slowly; the hours dragged. The pot of tea stayed warm and full. Bridie made three loaves of Killybegs brown bread, finally coming alive and participating.

Winnie made a nice, big Irish breakfast for our dinner. We gulped it down and were ready to leave at half-six. Brendan and Sean Turelli topped the car up with top-grade petrol, brushed out the interior and polished the windows.

We got in the car without a sound. I am comfortable with my rosary to cling to when I am anxious. Brendan drove at a steady rate, in full control of the wild horses under the bonnet.

Deirdre got out of the car, talked to the attendant, and he pointed where he wanted us to park. Brendan parked, left the motor running for the heat. Sean accompanied Deirdre to the hillock above the Cliffs of

Moher. The wind could have lifted the both of them up and tossed them into the sea.

Sean stood sentry as Deirdre and I made for the Ladies Loo. "Oh, Fiona," she whispered, "can you believe all this so soon?"

When Deirdre reached Sean, she pointed to the sea at Liscannor, to show him what she saw. They ran back to the car, Brendan negotiated the parking lot, the fast-moving traffic, and the hidden overgrown boreen that rolled down to the sea.

The big ship made a slow, 360-degree turn, and the *Maid of the Midst* was headed toward shore, out about ten miles. It was strangely quiet – no Garda, no lovers, no families, or fishermen. Just the four of us hidden beside a huge, black bolder down on the strand.

As Anne Marie came close to shore and the long pier, her yacht low in the water with fresh cut cocaine in tightly packed white bulk wrap, someone shouted "GO" and the beach was flooded with light.

Sargent Paul Foley shouted through a bull-horn, "Come Ashore! This is Garda Foley. We have a force waiting to arrest you and the gang of Dashes with you! Do not resist!"

Deirdre and Brendan ran out from behind the boulder to stand beside Paul. She could not wait to see the expression on her face. Anne Marie steadied her Glock 24 and aimed it straight at Deirdre.

Brendan pushed Deirdre down into the sand as the bullet caught him in the neck. The force of it blew Brendan back on his heels and he landed on top of Deirdre.

"Brendan," whispered Deirdre, "you've landed on top of my new baby, your grandchild!"

Brendan squeezed Deirdre's hand and expelled his last breath. Anne Marie fired again at Deirdre, as an FBI bullet from Ronan's Glock 19 hit her, lifting her small body high in the air and down into the rough, black waters, right in the path of her untamed yacht.

A voice that Deirdre knew well, shouted, "You're under arrest! The FBI is arresting you!"

As the last life force expelled from Brendan, Deirdre looked up and saw her brother, Ronan Flaherty, aiming at the Dashes. He aimed at his father and his bullet tore through Joe Dashes chest.

The other two Dashes were trying to protect their drugs, but Ronan's bullets tore up their inflatable dinghies and they went flying into the cold and dark waters of the Atlantic, cocaine falling from the sky like fresh Christmas snow.

Paul Foley pulled Brendan off Deirdre and lay beside him, his young head on his father's still chest.

Epilogue

There is a Time for Every Season

Sister Winnie O'Grady lived out her final years in great love and contentment. She spent hours in their little chapel, constructed by Jack Kelly and his team, and dedicated to Father Garrett Kelly and Father Brendan Foley. She drew her last breath on May 9, 2028 in the middle of the night.

Garrett Kelly was both jeered and respected, even loved, as his popularity grew. Young seminarians, both male and female, sought to learn more of the Covenant faith that informed Garrett's life.

Deirdre Flaherty Foley had twin daughters, six months after the Dragon Lady and the three Dashes were put out of business. Together with her husband, Captain Paul Foley, they had many children who could read, speak, and write in Irish, as spoken on the Aran Islands. The first boy was named Brendan Foley, after his grandfather.

Lily Flaherty grew to be a determined little dynamite, just like her mother. She would put up with no non-sense from the little ones. Lily joined the Garda and became very critical of her father who had taught her all she knew. She was demoted by the Garda and learned to listen to her father.

Gino Turrelli and his seven sons went back to their community and moved out to Lake Forest, a wooded suburb north of Chicago. The boys soon married and, stayed within a mile of their father. The many, many Turelli grandchildren kept Papa Gino busy and happy for the rest of his life. He never remarried.

Jerry Muldoon suffered waves of revulsion and shame over his sister's crimes. All of the money that had come to him through her illicit drug selling went to Catholic Charities. He went to Chicago with Pat Flaherty, stayed with him for a few months in his condo looking over Lake Michigan. Jerry sat on a bench in Lincoln Park and a young man asked if he could sit at the end of the bench. His name was Harry Harrington, a former priest. Jerry and Harry were together for the next 28 years, until Jerry had a massive heart-attack on the 4th of July.

Nurse Anne Smyth was anxious to retire, but instead, she and her husband, Tom Smyth, took over the responsibilities for the Gilhooly place. Tom was a gifted man about the place and never let it grow old. His wife was the general manager, nurse, and counsellor. They hired a cook, a cleaner and a general hired hand to help Tom as they continued to love and extend the place.

The place was dedicated by Winnie and Fiona, and all the people who helped them and by the guests that were present. It was given the name of *Gilhooly's Garden*, because all who entered there were destined to grow. They had a small, permanent sign above the door: *Expect a Miracle.*

Bridie Farrell continued to live contentedly at Gilhooly's Garden for the rest of her life. She began a small garden in the back that grew exponentially each year. Bridie and Winnie never suffered a cross-work between them.

William Campbell came to their door and inquired if Bridie Farrell was in residence. Being restless the night that the thatched cabin went up in flames, he climbed up the far side of Iron Mountain. When he could see the family cabin, it was simply ashes and soot. He knew his parent were gone, as well as his brothers and sisters. He had often heard rumors about an old woman on the roads with her big dog.

Professor Mary Agnes Mulvihill had a supreme nervous breakdown. She and Anne Marie Muldoon had been together since they were five. Her betrayal was like a ton of sand that continued to fall in her face. The dean suggested she go to Silver Hill in New Cannan, Connecticut, for a rest. She fell in love with her psychiatrist and he had already fallen in love with her. She never returned to Ireland.

Ronan Flaherty kept his position with the FBI. In addition, he was hired on to the Garda and to Interpol. Like his uncle Pat Flaherty, he never married. He kept homes in Kilrush, Chicago and Lyon, France. His focus was the extermination of drugs and the gangs that lived off them.

Sister Fiona Flaherty, Oh, who me?? I still write books.

Books by Kathleen FitzGerald

Brass: Jane Byrne and the Pursuit of Power

The Good Sisters

Whatever Happened to the Good Sisters? (ed.)

Alcoholism: The Genetic Inheritance

Women in A.A. (ed.)

Tales from the Titanic:

Figures of Speech: The Official Handbook

Martin: An Authentic Priest in a Time of Chaos

Gypsy Rovers

Available for purchase at Amazon.com.
Paperback: $12.95.

Kindle: $8.95

Made in the USA
Monee, IL
03 September 2020